Lives and Minds of C.W. Männe

BINGE

CHRISTOPHER WILLIAM MAHNE
SIR DAVID MICHAEL ROBINSON

BRAINIAC

PRODUCTIONS, LLC

TO MY BELOVED MUZZY, WHO TAUGHT ME TO FEAR
NOTHING, AND

TO MY MOTHER WHO CONTINUES TO SHOW ME
HOW TO LIVE LA VIDA LOCA,

THANK YOU AND I LOVE YOU ALWAYS!

C. W. Männe

Photograph by Estevan Oriol
Lettering by Mister Cartoon

Repeat...
Death.
Forgiveness.
Consciousness.

Repeat...
Death.
Forgiveness.
Consciousness.

Repeat...
Death.
Forgiveness.
Consciousness.

Repeat...
Death.
Forgiveness.
Consciousness.

PROLOGUE

n that gloom of chartreuse, which was the color of fluorescent lights upon indifferent walls, the breeze through my window had done its part to comfort me in my final moments, delivering upon it, a thousand tiny treasures. As it cockled through the soft curtains at my window, ruffling their delicate hems, I was reminded of a thousand Summer dresses, upon as many Summer girls, all those years down the shore. Too, there was a collage of vernal scents, which delivered with it a merciful provision of memories. The pale scent of a woman, hanging linens on a line; the optimism of embering, afternoon charcoals; and, best of all, one last yellow drift of Carolina Jessamine, the flower that had cast the signature perfume over my life. All of that joy, smuggled within the coin purse of a breeze, past those resigned doctors and nurses just outside, to that place where I lie in bed. It is possible, that I imbued sentimental fragrances upon a neutral wind, but, I assert, that was the prerogative of the dying.

And, in that nostalgic midst, I discovered one new companion, who had made safe passage across that window's sill and into my room. I was captivated by the mystery of his ascent to that high place, marveling at how he had managed such a grainless wall without the least bit slipping. And then, how he had done the thing of inverting his stripes, fastening himself upside down in that silent corner, which I thought reserved for cobwebs and long legged spiders alone. It was mere hours earlier he'd begun the mysterious enterprise, of transforming from caterpillar to chrysalis. At last, he appeared to pull the covers over his wriggling head, and disappeared completely into that tiny sock, where I alone had seen him.

As if upon that cue, my last companion arrived and caused a modest commotion amongst the gathered staff at my door, who had begun collecting as a confederacy of ghouls, indicating that my time was nigh. Anunk had that stirring affect wherever he appeared, for unlike that discrete caterpillar, Anunk was not a man to be hid. He was a shocking sight in any land, but his own, for there was no negotiating one's eyes from the prodigious plume of his yellow-white hair, which covered the deepest blackness of his face. That great mane, which had never known the sweep of brush or comb or shear, formed a silvery proscenium arch beneath which stood the marvelous character of his face. The high places upon him, which were his brows, his cheeks, his nose and chin, were each pressed and wide-set, cast in the stocky rubber of his flesh. Each of those wonderful crests upon him, served to make deeper, each dark crease, until those deep lines came to form a cursive scripting into the very face of him.

BINGE

Never had a time passed in his presence, when I hadn't thought how much I loved those sweeping and symmetrical esses, which were cast from the wings of his nostrils to become the mezzanine beneath his cheeks. Anunk was a timeless and magnificent man. From the earliest clay upon this earth, I was certain, Anunk had been cast, some several centuries before.

He set down the few things he carried on his person, as well as the large cane instrument, which rivaled him in height. My nurse, a sweet woman, had become increasingly alarmed by Anunk's activities, and worked to retard his progress. I communicated consent with my eyes, to which she finally submitted, leaving Anunk and me alone in that room.

Anunk quickly closed the door behind her, leveraging a chair up under its knob, so that it could not be opened again. He then took my face into his ancient hands, adjusted it so that my eyes were completely locked with his. He peered deeply into me, his eyes sparkling as dravite, broadcasting that singular color that is hidden in that stride between the step from rust to russet.

He reached into his haversack, from which he retrieved a thermos and a small wooden cup, setting them each on the bedside table. Next, he produced and lit an enormous cigar. With his weathered hands, he covered my face, forcing my eyelids to close. He then began a chanting, as he built a great brume of smoke over the whole of me...

BOOK ONE
"Time & Forgetting"

CHAPTER 1

SUBTERRANEAN

 was a prisoner of deep sleep, only the least bit of consciousness had diluted an otherwise perfect leaden state. I hovered there in lucidity, as long as I was able, a discipline I had hard won through a life committed to oversleep. My favorite time of day, save that of climbing into bed, had always come with the rise of my consciousness from its deep pit of slumber. As if a sun cresting the eastern horizon, my wakefulness first appears to me as a precise and thin horizon of light, projected upon the interior of my closed lids. At last, that golden thread of light always dissolves, as if it were a filament of sugar, consumed by an ever inferior alertness. It is precisely there, where sleep and wakefulness brush each other at dawn, that I have accumulated these delicious ounces of heaviness, which have become the richness that now lines the pockets of my mind.

In rare, but wonderful moments, where I have been able to emerge from sleep by the slowest of degrees, I have been enveloped in the sense of my connection to every living thing. Somehow, just moments before reason has found its purchase in me, the magical realism that governs dreams has delivered to me moments of pure identification with my soul.

On that morning, I had landed deftly on the image of myself as a tiny vine, unfurling at dawn in a vast Colombian Amazon. My involuntary tendrils set forth as tiny soldiers in search of arriving light, while my tapped roots stretch oppositely, like pirouetted toes in search of a morning drink. Whatever the case, the depth of my sleep was profound and I was pocketing a few grams of the gift that sleep alone can bring.

It would all have been perfect, had it not been for a growing sharpness in my throat. I had felt such sharpness before, which I knew to be a symptom of profound thirst, and so, I attempted mightily to swallow. I was unable, as if paralyzed somehow. Something was profoundly amiss, as I discovered the circuit between my mind and the whole of me was somehow broken. My thoughts and my actions were no longer connected, but worse, at odds with one another.

As moments passed, without relief, I deduced unhappily that the back of my mouth, where my throat and pallet met, was an ever decreasing aperture. The rapidly closing hole was the

BINGE

result of failing glands and a swelling tongue, which worked with unified purpose, in a suffocating campaign. At last, the easement between my lips and lungs had become like a dark column of razors, which I could not relieve.

My preoccupation with thirst, however, was to be quickly eclipsed by an even more pressing requirement, which was to find some bit of oxygen to delay my certain and impending doom. The realization of depleting oxygen, had begun an instinctive mental countdown, which precipitated the rationing of my high breath. My mind fumbled drunkenly to understand the nightmarish conditions into which I had awakened. At last, unable to determine the nature of my confinement, nor to affect my physical oppression by force of will, I cowardly concluded that I should retreat to the safety of sleep. Perhaps, thought I, my wakefulness had not yet consumed my waning slumber; a slumber, which would insulate me from that tunnel of horror. Within seconds, which I could not spare, the folly of my thinking was revealed. The gravity of my wakefulness had so asserted itself upon me, that my mind was trapped in its woeful orbit.

As if Death required any further compromise of my acuity, a parade of searing pain signals began traversing my dying trunk. Beginning as hundreds of tiny needles in the arches of my feet and the volars of my palms, jagged capsules of pain raced through me, converging into my center chest. I felt each individual pain as a carbonated shard rising through a poisoned bloodstream.

Ultimately, the aggregating pains clamored for space inside my failing lungs, until, at last, I was certain I would burst.

Briefly, then, those pains unified into a consolidated mass, which suddenly collapsed into itself, and then exploded in a mushroomed agony through the entirety of me. That great eruption carried such outward force that I felt the evacuation of my very self. The pain had somehow leeched across the membrane between my sinew and spirit, becoming like a sword through my soul. I was no longer human...no longer a multiplicity of feelings, desires or ambitions. I was but one comprehensive thing: I was Pain.

I believe it was then when I attempted to open my eyes, which sounds a strange thing to have waited so long to do, but upon reflection, all that I have recounted thus far was a series of seconds, which merely seemed a lifetime. I found resistance upon my eyes, which was a soft and insistent weight, which prevented me from opening them. I shuddered violently, only to discover that the weight on my eyes was equaled by a weight distributed over the whole of me, akin to a blanket of lead. It was, in fact, an earthen tarp, and I realized, conclusively, that I was NOT in the clutches of a night terror. I was in the most horrifying moment that may follows dreams, where I reached the worst of all possible conclusions: I was alive, underground!

BINGE

CHAPTER 2

EXTREMITIES

s I sought my dimming mind urgently for some option, I realized that the violence of my shuddering was having a small impact, as particles of dirt fell around me and the weight upon me was becoming somewhat... lighter. I focused all of my remaining being on raising my head, as a swimmer surfacing from an unknown depth, resisting the compulsion to breathe deeply. At last, my lungs were ablaze with burning sugars, as my body consumed the last of itself.

It was just then, when the dirt above my face was but a veil, that a provision of cool air found me. I was near the surface, but I still did not have the clearance to breathe, thinly encased as I was. One premature breath, thought I, would carry with it a cork of earth, which would seal my throat, silencing me forever. With a final stretch of my neck, I at last breached the earth and took a deep plunging breath! As soon as that small ration of oxygen made its way through my wilted esophagus, it was urgently distributed to the outskirts of me.

The sweet relief, which came only a second or two before my doom, I shall never forget. Upon recalling that moment, even now, I can see the rouging in the flesh of my forearms, in response to this deepest memory of mine. For certain, since that moment and have never taken for granted the generous gift of oxygen in the ambient around me. I find myself constantly accounting, inventorying the quantity of air around me. Unmarried, I suppose I consider oxygen the way another man considers his wife and children, as the center point around which his life is ordered. It is worth mentioning, that I am equally captive to the horror that proceeded the moment of salvation, which has left me profoundly claustrophobic and an apathetic gardener.

As my head was borne from the earth, it must have appeared to all of surrounding creation, as a great cabbage exploding from the ground. As I blinked away the dirt and gave myself some minutes to appreciate the gift of my own life, I also became fully alert. Through dusted eyelashes and a face caked in clay, I surveyed what I could, which led to several strange observations.

Chiefly, while my head was above ground, there was no sign, whatever, of the rest of me. I searched eagerly, my head on a swivel, until I briefly concluded that I had survived a beheading. I had no sensation of my extremities, since I breached the ground;

not even that phantom feelings of a trunk or limbs. I felt only my round head resting on a short neck, peering into the strange and never before seen surroundings.

As my thinking distilled, less parts desperation, more parts reason, I concluded that it was unlikely that mine had been the first head to survive a divorce from the body. As any investigator might do, I began collecting clues, premised on the given that my body was somewhere below that ground.

As I did finally make contact with the sensation in my extremities, I was able to wiggle my toes, such that some earth was moving about two meters forth of me. I was horizontal thank God. It may sound trivial, but had I been stuck in the earth as a post, I concluded that I should never have been able to unearth myself.

As my mind began to run the physical circuit, to discover the full nature of my encasement, I discovered to my added horror, that my hands were fastened together AND that they were behind me. That moment made true the maxim, "He who increases knowledge, increases suffering," for upon the realization that I was hog-tied, my shoulders began a searing and synchronous dull ache, heightened by light haze of burning.

For what must have been an hour, I worked my body back and forth, up and down until my chest was above ground. At last, with one final push of force, I shot forth from the ground like a javelined asparagus. I landed face down and panting, which produced a plume of dust about my head, as I had landed upon scorched earth.

CHAPTER 3

IRRECONCILABLE DIFFERENCES

s I looked to the hammocked spot of earth, where I had been entombed, I discovered at its end, a small cross made of sticks, around which hung a colorful beaded necklace. As my eyes blinked into focus, it was not a necklace, at all, but rather, a vest of some kind. Thousands of tiny beads had been woven in a heavy mosaic, the result of which was the arresting face of a jaguar.

The fusion of blacks, oranges, greens and umber, made the vest look almost liquid. Presently, however, I found myself captivated by two inset stones, where the cat's eyes were located. Unlike the beads, the eyes were jewels, which shimmered with a deep amber that I can only describe as 'bottomless'. Those eyes were increasingly hypnotic on me, and so I stared and stared into them, not moving for some time. I could feel some kind of invisible rope connecting me to that creature's eyes.

As I meditated upon those deep-set gems, I processed the conflicting clues that I had collected, which I could not resolve one to another. Given my shallow planting, horizontal, I assumed that had been buried in haste. My hands and feet bound, I could only assume that I had been taken by great force—overcome. Further, given that I had survived underground, I could only conclude that whatever the events, I had been murdered, which murderers had just fled.

However, there was the conflicting evidence of that cross and ornamental vest. Both symbols that my death had been ceremonialized. Both indicated that my death had meaning to someone. How could it be that I had been both murdered AND honored in my death? This irreconcilable difference in the nature of my demise, would prove to be one of many such conflicts, which were part of the foundational logic for the macabre world into which I had been born.

As the sun dashed the sky, I became aware of a long shadow, which was stretching itself incrementally across the face of me. Still bound, I looked to the object casting that shadow and discovered another cross! Around that primitive crucifix hung a garland of colorful feathers, like those of a headdress. It was another fresh grave, adjacent to mine!

BINGE

Any peace then dissolved from me, as I writhed wildly to free myself from the crude constraints about my wrists and feet. Once freed, I clawed my way across the earth, digging furiously into that shallow grave. Preeminent, were the thoughts of some cohort of mine, who was expiring thereunder, as I had so narrowly avoided. I felt the layers of flesh tearing away my fingertips and the explosion of my cuticles, until, at last, my fingers were as rags. To my horror, I discovered myself too late for my underground companion.

Revealed there, the yawning face of horror that I had unearthed, was that belonging to a woman of great years. She was eighty years old, if she was a day, and her face was in the tableau of a silenced scream. Caked in dirt, her eyes were open and frozen, as if the last they beheld was some demon from hell, come to take her life. "I'm so sorry," I said, "I didn't know. I didn't know."

I didn't recognize her, which served to further my confusion. This was not a woman of whom I had any knowledge. Curiously, given all the horror to cope with in that moment, I became superficially transfixed. There, in that trough of doom, beneath the dust and ashes upon that old woman, I caught a glint. Yielding, just briefly, to ensure no necrophilial offence, I reached for the charm, dusting it free with my thumb and forefinger. The newly minted fossil was that of a Saint Christopher medallion.

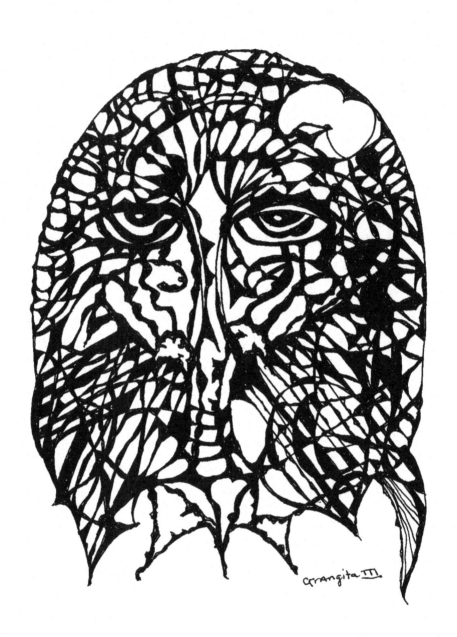

Upon contact with that trinket, a sentimental spear shot through the center of my mind, as if the medallion had carried with it a secret current. I felt a connection with that charm, which I could not negotiate. I was overwhelmed with the impulse to collect it for myself, only temporarily restrained by the revulsion at my own baseness. The impulse in me was so strong, however, that with hypnotic movement, I released the chain from behind the dead woman's neck and fastened it about my own. I can say that as I did this, it was simultaneously against my nature and congruent with my will.

Whether the result of my cardinal sin or some yet realized cause, my temperature spiked and the world around me became a darkling tunnel. As the charm rested there upon my chest, the great irony was not lost on me, that Saint Christopher was the patron saint of travelers.

CHAPTER 4

THE CLEARING

 s I blinked into consciousness again, I awakened with no memory of my fainting, nor knowing how long I had been out. The sun had traveled some distance in the sky, indicating that I had spent many hours in sleep. My best guess is that it was midday.

From that recumbent position, the world emerged again to me, though horizontally. The landscaped view served immediately to aggravate my already turgid bowel. As my head rolled into a traditional upright position, I discovered that the fluid of my inner ears moved on a short delay, such that I was awash in vertigo. This was an incrementally negative development for the condition of my gut, as discomfort was stacked and then stacked again.

Through my nausea, I took inventory of what I could around me, ordering my analysis of the place, moving from its outermost edges, inward. I was in a clearing of some kind, a plateau which was fenced in all direction by a thriving jungle vitality; an ocean of trees, which created a viridescent bluff around my camp. The clearing was no more than fifty meters square, so that I concluded I had been abandoned in some deep part of the jungle.

Most prominent of my subsequent observations, save the two earthen coffins in which my companion and I had been buried, there was a very large cistern. The iron cauldron was a meter high and heavily used. As I gazed at it from my short distance, I could see that it was still throwing from its great circumference, a heat signature, muddling the view of everything behind it. It was still warm to the touch when I inspected it for contents, and I was arrested by an emergent odor, the likes of which I have never encountered.

My thirst was complex, so no matter the smell, thought I, this was the only sign of hydration. It's being heated gave me hope that it was some form of nutrient and that it had been sterilized. And so, I cupped that sedimentary brew into the palm and took a long draught, choking on it as I imagined it to be the swill of a jackal's dung. I admit in the swallowing, I believed that I would either be rescued from thirst or that I had finally drunk my death. Either outcome, in those moments, was agreeable. The foulness ran down my throat like thick paint, forming heavy fingers, which soldiered into the hollow pit of me.

𝕭𝕴𝕹𝕲𝕰

Within moments, even the fuel from that fetid drink allowed the recovery of my senses, chiefly that which I desired least, which was my full sense of smell. It was no longer the simple fume of that drink, but something much more offensive prowling in the ambient around me. This was not a simple note, but a symphony of stink, that would not be ignored.

As I searched the place further, I unhappily discovered at the perimeter of the clearing, in every direction, a multiplicity of human waste. There were the vilest contents, laying unabsorbed in shallow pits about the camp. The shallow holes were some kind of temporary toilets, I concluded, which must have served a dozen men, sick men. There is no way to recall it with honesty and not just say each hole was brimming with vomit and shit, and in most cases, blood. If this had not been the work of a dozen men, it was certainly the work of one man for a year.

A few moments amongst those rising vapors, assisted by the memory of that stagnant water which I had drunk, and my body began a comprehensive purging, evacuating me from every opening. Every toxic thing, whether liquid, solid or spirit, was projected from me in columns of fire. The crusade to expel the full inventory was unrelenting for a little over a minute. And then, against expectation, I had the most wonderful feeling.

I felt a cool pillar of light from above me, which was more the character of the moon than sun. The light seemed to cradled me into it and brought me to a perfect rest. I was in one second ejecting in every possible way, in agony, and then in the adjacent moment, I was filled with the kind of health I had never felt before. It was as if I had never been sick in a lifetime, was I so separated from any feeling of discomfort. I don't know how to explain it, except to say it was a kind of perfect physical peace. I was simply, well. I was better than well, I was strong. This condition made as much sense to me as anything else I had encountered in the place.

The sun made haste in its decline, but I had thankfully discovered that beneath that cauldron was a breath of white smoke. The drifting spiral was a thread, which led to a faintly glowing haystack of timbers, which I was able to stoke, just as the sun fell suddenly, like a great yellow marble from a table's top.

Whatever that place, my first day had been completed there, ending suddenly, as God's great fingers pinched the wick of the sun delivering me into darkness.

BINGE

CHAPTER 5

THE JAGUARED EDGE

 was encompassed comprehensively and two-fold. The first layer of shrouding around me was the pitchy darkness, which exerted itself upon me with the suffocating power of a closed fist. There is no better word to describe such an absolute void of light, as 'aphotic'. It was as dark as pitch. All of that eclipse was unrelieved by any iridescence, which might have shone, were it not for the misfortune of a new moon a-sky.

My fire proved but a stump, casting only an abbreviated radius of light about me and then ending abruptly, as it collided with the surging murk. As the fire slowly dwindled, the inky atmosphere slunk upon me as a rising unlit tide.

As quickly as the sun had fallen and my fire had faded, so too had the temperature dropped. By every falling degree, I became aware of a curious, and thereto overlooked, fact. In my panicked state, my assay had been prioritized from the outermost perimeter of trees and then moving inward to that tiny knot of fire, upon which I sat. I had stopped there, never having taken inventory of myself. Had it not been for the cold breath of night, which was whispering across my flesh, I should not have realized that I was completely naked!

In the intensity of my outward focus, I had never been aware of my full exposure. I mean no self-flattery to say it, but my oversized cock had proved a faithful companion in my life, warning me of the conditions around me, through its surging and retreating. I should have thought, looking back on it, that its constant swinging hither and yon, would have awakened me to my nakedness. Based on its presentation, the cold was not so great that I needed dress, but I concluded that I should, at least, protect my kit.

In the heap of trash near the cauldron, I foraged and found a rag, which I fashioned into a sort of loin cloth. It was really more of a pouch, which tethered my manhood into a consolidation and shot a thin rope across my taint and upward between the cheeks of my ass, where it was finally secured by leads across my hips. It was ingenious and I admit that the feeling was quite marvelous, as my collected anatomy made for a fine presentation, even in that darkness.

Pursuing the impulse further, I retrieved the wonderful beaded vest from my grave marker and donned it forthwith. I must have looked as much the primitive chieftain as any man

BINGE

before me, dressed as such and hunched over a waning fire. All of it was something of a paradox, for I was desperate and yet I was filled with this magnificent buzzing, to realize how wonderful it was to think myself a savage.

It was then, I was introduced to the second layer of my imprisonment. When my fire was finally out, I was enveloped by a true blackness, the likes of which I have never known. With all loss of sight, I was introduced to the latent dimension inside of darkness, which was its weight. Darkness, such as that infinite kind, has heft. It leans upon you, as if you are beneath the insistence of an ever expanding balloon. It plumes. It…it moves. It insists. More than swallowing you, the dark absorbs you in its path, stitching you up, until at last, you are alone in its pocket.

That darkness, however, was to become the junior of my anxieties, proving itself a mere accomplice to an approaching and genuine terror. Within that greater silence, the smallest of sounds carried like rifle shots through the still air. Some sounds were sensible, such as the crackling of the dying fire or the ruffling of birds in the adjacency or the rummaging of small creatures in the distal underbrush. Those sounds I could live with, as they were a part of my vocabulary. What was impossible, however, was to reconcile one nomadic sound.

The best and worst that I then did, was discern what that sound was, which was stalking me at the perimeter. In the presence of that migrating sound, all other sounds ebbed away, such that that...respiratory rattling...was all I could hear. The sound was as rhythmic as it was mobile. Hungry and low, it was a prowling sound. I was confident it was the breathing of a slow and methodical beast, which moved with the adeptness of experience. The sound in those lungs crackled and popped, and were distorted by reverberation inside the great throat of the beast. The creature had a sweeping advantage, as I was convinced by its easy movement, that it could see beneath the inky cloak of night. As if anything could have made it worse, the proximity of the sound was approaching me, as if on a tightening spiral track.

To flee in that darkness was certain death. I could not see my own fingers, let alone step in any direction. As much a coward as I feel to say it, I was forced to a total surrender, preferring to die there in that pitchy spot than to make a clown of myself, stumbling and screaming into the obscurity. I envied the relief of the sweet woman, laying only a few meters from me, as she had already done the hard work of dying, and was then enjoying the peace of dreamless sleep. In that moment, I would happily have traded souls with her.

So I spineless, sat. My high heart pressed against the ceiling, becoming a pulsing yoke in my throat. If there was a prayer then, it was simply that my death in the fangs of that beast would be dramatic and quick. And so, I sat, eyes like useless coils, alert and waiting.

BINGE

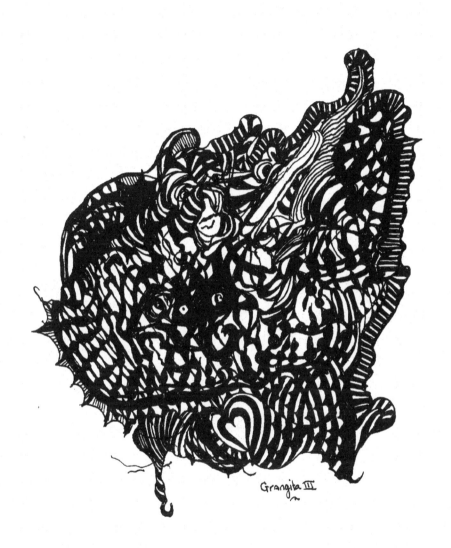

CHAPTER 6

SAVAGE

erhaps, thought I, the beast was deriving some pleasure from the hunt of me, extending the ecstasy of the kill by prolonging my life that night. Not a second of that night had passed, during which I had not believed each moment to be my last. I was so consumed in fear that I failed to recognize each passing moment had formed a bridge, which connected me, at last, to a rising dawn.

The morning light worked miracles in dissolving the powerful inertia which had anchored me through the night. Something about the light of day, as has always been the case, erased my fears and allowed for the rebuilding of a protective scaffolding around my mind. I dismissed the thoughts of death and loss and my profound weakness, replacing them with the deluded construct of security. Hope, in the end, is the noble lie I tell myself. For, as the great poet has asked, "Who amongst us has the courage to believe in nothing?"

In the depth of night, listening to the breath of that concealed fiend in the perimeter, I had pigeon-heartedly resigned myself to die in that spot, either of starvation or in the eye teeth of that barbarian. In such a moment as that, where control was hopelessly lost, I found some kind of comfort in choosing the manner of my death.

Further, there was a tug of war between the known and the unknown. To choose the manner of my death, gave me a strange calm. To confront the wilderness of an unlit jungle, even were it the possible road to safety, was too much for my undersized heart. In the end, I would rather have died there in that clearing than to have ventured into the dim unknown.

Daybreak, however, allowed me to rack my focus, so that I then saw the vast wilderness about me in all of its majesty. Rather than silhouetted demons, I now saw the lushness of a miraculous canopy. Instead of the deepset eyes of that predator, I saw the bursting of flora in an equatorial forest. And the sounds that haunted me through the gloom of night were now the music of heaven's manifold creatures. It was all so beautiful in the first light that I felt my strandedness a privilege.

It was decided for me: I would not remain tethered to that spot, nor would I run from the fangs of the invisible beast. If I were to die, it would be a glorious death, in which I was no longer prey, but predator. While my belly did not feel the sting

BINGE

of hunger, my mouth watered for the taste of a fresh kill. An impulse, for which I had no reference, was to sink my full face into the dying neck of that midnight stalker. There was, but to ready myself to enter the thrill of the hunt.

I had fashioned a makeshift spear, shaving the tip of a cane branch into a sleek point. With a hypnotic impulse, I tested the razored edge by cutting a small diagonal across my outer forearm, producing a thin signature of blood. The crimson gash provided a pallet for my fingers, which then brushed my face, so that I was alight in my own blood. With this final act of the warrior, my conversion to native man was complete. As the sweat of my brow began to commingle with the blood on my cheeks, my tongue darted eagerly to the corners of my mouth, where it caught the nectar, filling me with the taste of ore.

I felt the iron drifting through me, dusting the full column of my spine, as a wonderful geyser of rage rose through me. While the clearing provided no reflective surface, I can only imagine the horror that I presented to the world around me. I had been positively transformed.

Armed with my cane spear, bloody face and the Saint Christopher medallion, there was but one decision between me and whatever was to come inside that waiting jungle: where to enter the place.

My eyes were reduced to slits, as I peered decidedly into the one spot where I had last heard the breathing of that beast, just before sunrise. At the darkest point on the perimeter, just behind a thicket of low brush, there hung a curtain of creepers. Resolved, I would enter right there, where I had felt those amber eyes of the beast watching me. I would enter the vastness, precisely where my fear was most focused, and more importantly, where there was no path.

CHAPTER 7

QUARTER TIME

s I left the clearing, I peeled back the drapery of creepers, which hung there like the heavy braids from the head of a great monster. The ropey vines were slick and heavy, and as I pressed forth into the overgrowth, they swatted clumsily at my sides.

The first I observed, as I entered that landscape unlike any I had ever seen, was the pressing vitality. It was almost so lush as to be suffocating, for in all directions I was awash in technicolor nature. The thickset canopy above me was so dense that the tiniest points of sunlight were allowed to penetrate. The resultant ceiling appeared to me as a jade sky, filled with stars.

The trunks of trees were like colossal sculptures from the foundations of the earth, their great bowls meeting the primeval forest floor and sending forth craggy fingers to anchor their great heights. I imagined that to support such immense structures, the root systems beneath the ground must have extended hundreds of meters in all directions. Had I not felt small enough as it was, I certainly did then.

As vast as the place was, my aloneness there created a sort of intimacy, where I became aware of the subtle detail in plants that I had never considered before. Upon my slow and close inspection, I discovered that the luxuriant boscage was created by a perpetual layering of one species upon another. Each plant was like a voice, which produced a unique note, until the diversity sang together as a chorus of nature.

The skin of the trees was also the ground for thick mosses, which slickly painted the forest, creating opalescent flashes. Atop those mosses and in the fibrous gaps of trees, a thriving diversity of florets were fixed. Most prominent from my aspect, I was impressed by the teeming orchids. Strategically punctuating the tangle of vegetation, the patent volume of orchids brought relief to an otherwise verdant sea. I swear in that moment, I could see the fresh strokes of God's great fan brush, as each petal was still yielding beneath the weight of wet paint. In all cases, the family were of epiphytic orchids, whose corked roots were as nearly magnificent as their blooms. The sculptured roots grew above ground at elongated diagonals, trailing each bloom, until at last they appeared to me as the tails of efflorescent kites.

I found that I was no longer hurried or intense. My pulse and full faculties had been slowed to the wonderful quarter time of nature. Under the influence of this new meter, I became aware of other delights, which had thereto escaped me. Most entertaining of these was a small cadre of hummingbirds, which had plumed together to form a multi-colored cloud above my head. Following my every step, the tiny birds formed a whirring halo, as if connected to me by some profound, but invisible tether. Their tiny bodies bore a signature of color so unique, I can only think to describe them as having been washed in oil filled pomegranates. Like the wet petals of the flowers and the opalescence of the moss, so too were these hovering companions alight in dancing pigments.

Perhaps, what I loved even more than what I had seen in that place, was in what I had NOT seen. There was not, nor had there ever been, the hand of a gardener. It was a wonderful realization, to know that the beauty of the world was not made by man, but was the result of nature uninterrupted. And, that presumably, I was the only one to ever see it, the result of my entering that place where there was no path.

Something of that electric world was so comforting to my soul. The beauty of nature seemed to ground me in some way, which was through a total bypass of my rational defenses. Anxiety, only moments earlier, was the great fence around my mind, but upon being swallowed up in this natural wonder, my mind had been happily overcome. I suppose that I have never met the smuggler who is quite the equal to Beauty. For it was Beauty which had left me defenseless and allowed that deep calm to enter me, while I was so agreeably distracted. Whatever the case, the plants and that place exerted a spirit of deep well-being upon me, which under the circumstances, was the greatest testament to their power. The collaboration and harmony of that place, was due to the absence, not the presence, of man. As such, I counted myself an intruder there, and did my best to leave only the lightest footprints. Were that it had not just been true for me, which I discovered only three steps forth.

My sense of wonder was shattered by a bolt of terror, as I discovered a most horrifying thing upon the earth before me. In the trampled greenery, there was the carcass of a freshly mutilated ape. The creature was at least three quarters the size of me, so that it looked as much human as primate. It lie prostrate, it's limbs extending fully from its trunk, so that it took the tableau of a hairy starfish. I was disturbed enough by the presence of that half-human corpse, but my punctuated terror was aggravated further by the nature of its death.

Clearly, the body had been killed for the sake of killing alone and not the sake of food. Whatever beast had killed this poor creature was of enormous power and precision. I say precision because most disturbing of all on evidence there, was the anthropoid had been decapitated. The neck was a hollowed stump, from which was coursing a rhythmic stream of blood. Given the pulsing of that blood's exit, the heart in the thing was still faintly beating. Until, as I stood there watching, it stopped.

Upon close inspection, where the head had been separated from the pedestal of the neck, the cut was not ragged, as if ripped away. The cut bore witness to the skill of a surgeon or a tailor, as it was steady and exact. The freshness of that kill indicated its happening within meters of my standing, and yet, I had never heard so much as the rustling of a leaf. That monstrosity bore the mark of one predator alone: a man of stealth armed with a very sharp blade.

Paradise dissolved. And I... was no longer alone.

CHAPTER 8

DRAW

y terror was fleeting, quickly replaced by the resurgence of that blood-thirst. To have been so at ease in that natural beauty, only brought the vile brutality of man into a more keen focus. Moving from such a placid state into such revulsion, was an outright rape of my senses, which only furthered my resolve, as I was flushed with a new color of rage.

I made haste through the waist high grasses and vines, agnostic with respect to the source of blood. The hunger in me was not of the belly, but of the mouth. The mouth lives only for the taste of a thing; a noshing engine driven by cravings. In that moment, my lust was for the deep, sweet taste of flesh, and I would have my kill.

As I, determined, made my way, my exposed legs paid the high price of progress, as they were consistently brushed by the pointed nettles and nails of the low leaves, akin to the spears of aloe. Under the lashing of those plants, my lower body was in a swelling agony, but after some time, the pain grew to became... a delight. I actually found myself trying to amplify the sting, searching out the most jagged brush I could find. That pain was of that variety, which creates the compulsion for more of it. My legs came to bear the trophies of those myriad thorns, as the length of my calves and quadriceps became a canvass for a swarm of welts which came to cover them. Each unique point of contact, by the hundreds...by the thousands, formed individual white blisters upon my skin, until I was quite literally quilted in poison.

Just beneath the skin, the fury came to feel like a sexual itch, though I admit I found it more satisfying, as it was sustainable and unrelieved. That delicious pain was made perfect by an ether, which took residence in my head. The combination of sensations delivered me to such a state of ecstasy, that I was afloat over the ground, moving at high speed, so that the world around me became a great emerald blur.

Just ahead of me, appeared a streamlet, which was the first sign of water I had seen. The water flowed gently down the mild grade and eventually disappeared into a tall canebrake. As my eyes followed the serpentined creek, they came, at last, upon the magnificent object of their desire. There in the distance, I finally caught sight of the jet black frame with those deep-set amber eyes, sipping ignorantly from the stream. My mouth watered.

I took the habit of a jungle cat, moving with my head on a taught line, while my body beneath undulated with the terrain. Keeping my eyes level and moving with silent fluidity, I was, at last, within 20 meters of the oblivious cat. As I stalked, I worked to dry the dampness from my fingers, as I wrapped them tightly about the spear. Convinced that the whole of the forest could hear my heart beating, I did my best to relax my pulse and breathing, in every effort to retain the advantage of being undetected.

I raised my spear with a whisper and cocked the rolling hammer of my shoulder, readying myself for quick release. The distance was formally closed and I was so close that my nostrils were filled with the pungence of that fiend, who remained distracted at drink.

The lids of my eyes draped to the half-mast of sharp focus, I took a last breath in, and with no sound at all, I uncoiled and sent the great spear at the unknowing beast. As I watched the spike tightly spiraling the distance between us, I considered the consequences of being subsequently unarmed. To throw and miss was not only to throw my spear, but to throw the twin advantages of surprise. To not have thrown was the greater crime for a true savage. To be so comprehensively at risk, my future literally hung in mid-air between us. It was marvelous!

The spear was on a perfect trajectory and my eyes drew wide with the anticipation of the strike. In the final approach, however, the beast looked up and ducked the centimeters, which would have been its certain death.

More than a glancing strike, my cane found real purchase just above the cat's shoulder, cleaving a filet of muscle from its neck. The wound, however, was not lethal, which turned me from hunter to hare in an instant. It stared at me, generating that signature respiratory rattle, only then amplified by the adrenaline of counter attack!

When the demon caught sight of me, it roared with such a volume that I could see its breath running across the top of the high grasses between us. And, on the heels of that great sound, the cat sprung! As if launched from a secret catapult, its full, sleek sinew was in immediate flight of attack.

I raced the jungle for cover, my head like a gyroscope, knowing that I had no more than seconds to find cover. At last, I dove headlong into a densely laced thicket, where the tangle of fallen trees, had created a shallow alcove. I found myself secreted, my eyes peering through the stitching of branches that covered me. A panicked rabbit, I peered into the adjacency, where the cat was prowling.

The cat looked for me, it's chiseled proboscis raised high, as its sense of smell was far more useful in detection than sight. As frightened as I was, I couldn't help but admire how it moved with such an economy of motion; its head on a constant plane and its great black shoulders moving the elliptical path of coupling rods on a locomotive. Hungrily, it searched and then stopped. Taking a long draught of air, its jeweled eyes then registered the catch of my scent! It's black, stone head wheeling at a right angle to its length, locked eyes on my sheltered position.

Nothing then separated me from death, save the unknown strength of the bramble and my benediction. After a long stare, the cat leapt at full speed crashed into the serrated perimeter of my cave. Its great iron arms reaching in, swatting, I curled tightly into a ball, as far back in the hovel as I could press.

The eye teeth of that monster were dripping with spit and snot showered from its snout in all directions, until at last I was awash in a slick patina. As it surged over and over again, the heat of its lungs created an invisible column of fire that heated the bunker. In the troughs between each lusty breath, my own breath was lost to me. At last, came a gristling pop, the result of the creature's apparent and intentional dislocation of its own shoulder. The result: an extension of its reach by an additional half meter, until the separation between us was but an eyelash.

I was pressed against my limits, clawing as deeply into my position as I could do. My only option: to load my right leg in preparation for one great strike, which might catch the arm of the jaguar in such a way as to snap it in half. The sabled arm continued with a furious speed and determination. I took my chance thrust my leg forth, glancing against the creature's forearm. I had missed! In doing so, I had forfeited my position, my leg then fully extended like a ripe branch! The giant, wasted no time with its advantage, firing a ham-fist across my lower leg, scoring a deep staff into my flesh. The wash of fluids was then complete over me, as my own blood spilled like a slick of oil. I could but retreat to the deepest crevice, then badly wounded, but apparently, that eyelash out of reach.

The cat finally retired the kill, its tactics exhausted. The prowler had been splayed at the tip of my spear and I had been scored nearly to the bone by its razored claws. Our wounds were deep. We had both been permanently marked by the other; tattooed. But, in the end, our torrid exchange was a draw.

CHAPTER 9

FYLFOT

he jaguar had long dissolved into the forest, though I suspected he was biding his time somewhere in the silent tangle, waiting for me to emerge from that retreat. My wounds, while horrifying in appearance, were not so severe that I could not press on. My choice was no choice at all, really, for without the benefit of the spear, I would simply die in that briar.

As I surrendered my position and made way to recover the spear, I could feel an invisible band of safety, stretching taught and then finally snapping, as I reached fifty paces from the thicket. Should the cat have suddenly emerged there, there was too great a distance back to cover. Once beyond the boundary of safety, I moved with urgency to the place where my spear had struck the monster.

As I approached the streamlet, where I had cleaved the thing with my arrow, I came upon the deep, heavy footprints of the beast, where it had leaned forward to drink. The feet of that cat were a testament to its magnificent scale and made me consider that my makeshift pike was hardly enough to meet its great force. Like a child, I put my own foot into the muddy cast, and found that it was dwarfed by nearly a time and a half.

Knowing that the lancet had glanced off of the beast at a muted angle, I searched in the low mesh of trampled grass. As it happened, the spear was resting and in the open. I must say with the pride of a craftsman, it was in excellent condition, following its virgin strike.

The arrowed tip was filmed with a scarlet wash of blood, which was drying as paint. I touched it with the tip of my finger and found it to have the heavy viscosity of syrup, still warm to the touch. Unable to resist it, I unfurled my tongue and ran it the length of the arrow's flat sides, ingesting the ichor with hedonistic delight. As the claret from that beast ran down my throat, I could feel the vibrating roar of that creature, as if I had, instead, ingested its spirit. Spear at my side, the hours-devours of blood on my lips, I then caught a rustling at the top of a distant canebrake. The movement was only a half a klick forth, at a two o'clock aspect. It was most certainly the cat!

I was alight at once, running headlong into the danger, when all reason should have taken me in the opposite direction. Something about that animal's blood, perhaps, the proximity of death itself, and I was drunk with the impulse to either live free or die! The electrolytic infusion of that dull juice had created a deep footing in me, that one or the other of us should perish that day.

As I ran the landscape, floating the undergrowth, I was aided by a slight downhill grade. I was in pure pursuit of that low demon, all of the world around me reduced to a point of singularity in the form of that jet black silhouette, waiting somewhere in the distance.

I must have run for thirty minutes, never short of breath, only more intoxicated. I could no longer see evidence of the beast moving in the vegetation, eventually becoming, as he was, completely dependent on my sense of smell. The brute had a savory musk, which was distinct, but was also dissolving with each step that I took, until, at last, I lost all trace of him to the perfumed jungle.

I sat upon my haunches, leaning against the bowl of a tree that stretched into the foreverness of a hidden heaven above me. I had time to reflect on how deeply into the jungle I had surged. I had no way of knowing where I was or how I might ever return to the clearing. From where I was at rest, I was surrounded in all directions by an ocean of plants. I felt certain that I had reached the very epicenter of the bush.

I discovered a queer evidence, on level with my head, carved into the tree upon which I was leaning. Deeply scored into the flesh of that trunk, there was a strange marking. As I studied it, the shape became visible. It was an equilateral cross, bent at right angles, in a clockwise expression. Of course, I knew the symbol at once. It was the fylfot. The hakenkreuz. Der swastika.

What an impossible symbol to find in the center of a vast, uninhabited jungle. No beast had carved that, but man. A shot of hope ran through me, eclipsed quickly by an anvil of dread. Hope, in the idea that someone had been there before me and that I might not be completely lost. Dread, in the memory of that decapitated ape, which was clearly the victim of a great blade. A great blade, which may have hewn the fylfot before me.

I ran my fingers into the seams of the symbol, which produced a flash of electricity through me, as if it were a conduit of some kind. The current was much the same as that which had galvanized me upon contact with the Saint Christopher medallion, which I had discovered on the old woman.

As my fingers rested there, I closed my eyes and saw a sequence of wonderful, dancing lights. The longer my hand remained there, the more the feeling was like a tonic, which sent relief to every part of me. The stinging in those welts, the gashes in my legs, the pulsing of my heart were all... relieved.

When I opened my eyes again, I could see that all of the trees around me were scored with similar markings, though in one grove the symbol was clockwise and in the other, counter clockwise. Presently, I fastened my hand to the counter-clockwise symbol upon one of the trunks and was given another charge. As serene and wonderful as the first current was, the counter-clockwise current was its diametric opposite. My mind was assailed by a hurricane of darkly colored shards. Blacks, indigos, reds... other colors of violence showered me, as if a stained glass window had exploded. I withdrew my hand involuntarily, as if from a burning stove.

I was between poles of some kind. At one side, a path of markings with a positive charge; at the other, a negative charge. It occurred to me that the symbols on the trees may have been as arrows, creating opposing paths, of which one must be taken. That I, must then, choose a direction. I, of course, choose the positive path. And so, I set forth.

I was but fifty meters on that aspect, when something occurred to me, which if true, suggested there was another way.

CHAPTER 10

THE PINWHEEL

ith urgency, I retreated again to the fork of trees, where those paths had diverged. It had occurred to me if that if I was amidst some kind of charged field, perhaps the jungle itself was a kind of circuit. If such were the case, the whole of that place might, in fact, contain a third field; a ground field...a neutral path.

Upon my further assay, there were, in fact, only two paths from the place. But, there was something new that caught my attention, as I studied the fork more closely. I discovered an unorthodox collection of vines, which I had originally dismissed as the curved border of a jungle cul-de-sac; the natural dead end which divided those two paths. The creepers there bore a most curious trait. The vines did not descend from the high canopy of the jungle, but instead, ascended. These vines were not creepers at all, but climbers. Furthermore, the vines were distinct, unlike any I had seen during my time in jungle. As I rummaged through them, inspecting, I uncovered a most inconceivable thing.

There, behind that scrim, was the stump of a long fallen tree, back-dropped by a glowering darkness. Stuck into the pedestal, standing at full attention, was a child's pinwheel! The structure of the pinwheel was in the tradition of those which have filled the memories of children through the ages. It took the character of a flower, where the long, thin handle formed the stem and the petals were represented by an origami fan. However, unlike the sweet, multi-colored petals of a pinwheel, the petals of that pinwheel where formed by the layering of two swastikas, one in a clockwise orientation and one in the counter.

I plucked the grim toy from the soft stump, which led to a further discovery. The gadget had been planted, dead center, in the middle of these strange instructions: "SCHLAG UND BRUMMEN". While I had no idea who I was or where I was or how I might ever escape that world, I then discovered myself bilingual. I fluently interpreted the whittled expression from German to English, as, "Blow and hum."

As I raised my eyes to look beyond the stump, I was met with a plume of darkness. It was some kind of passage, but the way inside was unclear beyond a few meters or so. From what I could see, the dim view was created by a lushness of brush and vegetation, which grew wildly on all sides of it, so that it formed a sort of corridor. Additionally, the ground dropped off at a steep grade, which in concert with enclosure of that pressing growth, looked as much a rabbit hole as a pathway.

Taking a few steps forth, to gain view, for as far as I could see into it, the perspective of distance served to create the illusion of a tightening iris, as if I were peering through the end of a straw. While the illusion was only optical, it served to activate my new and acute claustrophobia.

As I think of myself in that moment, there I was, aboriginal, peering into a jungle straw and holding a macabre variety of pinwheel. Adding to that freakish collage, I returned my gaze to the instructions in the stump, reminded to 'blow and hum'. I held the pinwheel before me, blowing gently, which initiated the spinning of the two swastikas. As they gained speed, spinning in opposing directions, their sharp right angles dissolved, as did their unique characters, until their combined expression was that of a circle, which was bespoke, like a spinning wheel.

I blew as hard and as long as I could, increasing the spin of the wheel. At last, it was moving so fast that the wagon wheel effect began, so that the spokes of the circle appeared to oscillate, moving backward and then forward and backward again. The swastikas had long dissolved away and I became transfixed by a wonderful illusion, until my eyes surrendered to the mode a relaxed stare.

The combination of breathing and focus, put me in a state of repose, in which I remembered the second instruction. And so, I began to hum.

As I hummed a very strange thing began to happen to the image at the center of that spinning wheel. Something in the tone of my humming, served to change the behavior of the spokes before me. As I refined the modulation of my humming, a still image began to emerge. At last, my sustained pitch brought the frozen image into sharp focus: It was an elongated, horizontal figure eight; the mathematical symbol for infinity!

The exercise had activated a compulsion loop in my mind, such that I was exhausting myself to hold the view steady. I modulated just slightly higher to the figure eight so that it disappeared completely, creating a transparent window!

Through that window, I saw deeply into the corridor. Deep in that darkness I discovered a tiny pinhole of light. As I continued breathing and humming at that frequency, the light at the end of the tunnel slowly took the signature form of a lotus. The shape pulsed with spectral color, holding me in its gaze for a very long while, until I was forced, at last, to surrender to light-headedness.

I had found it. The third way. The hidden way. A neutral path that ran between the pairs of opposites.

CHAPTER 11

SHEEP SHANKED

 few steps into the corridor and I discovered that my initial courage had all of the substance of carnival candy, dissolving in the precise moment it was to deliver its promise. Even just those few strides in, the deep compression of the place activated a negative sense memory of my being buried alive. The jungle density hanging from the low ceiling was like navigating a gauntlet of monkey paws, each swatting at my face as I pressed forward, slicking me with their moisture. The dread in me rose persistently with each step that I took into the depth, and while I knew the tightening around me was simply an illusion, it was real enough to trigger the onset of a modest hyperventilation. Had it not been for the troth of that pulsing flower in the distance, I know that my claustrophobia would have trumped all, and I would have made hasty retreat.

My spear's extended character made it the excellent double for a machete, so in order to tame the effects of my panic, I methodically cut through the hanging vegetation, increasing my headroom. Pruning away at those vines, as I encountered them, created a wonderfully repetitive rhythm, which became as a powerful meditation. Something of the repeated movement and the coordinated breathing, helped to lower my pulse rate. The blade of my spear proved of such severity, that the vines melted easily at its edge, so that my passing was near effortless. At last, I gained some degree of ease, by finally resolving that the worm hole was simply a melodramatic hiking trail.

The inventory of vines was far too many to count, covering the full spectrum, I suspect God carries in his divine quiver. Vines of every color and density and behavior, wore the outward disguise of collision. But, within the forced intimacy between us, I came to understand that there was a collaborative stitch work of design. While most were versions of green, the vines were frequently punctuated by flashes of cork and rust. When viewed as a whole, the distance of the passage, the teeming formed a marvelous herringbone. The vines worked together to become a forest calligraphy; a coiled wallpaper, which braided the length of the place.

I continued to cleave my way, though my increased respect for the plants gave rise to greater discrimination. It was mid-shaft I came upon the most unique and magnificent vine, so wonderful that it stopped me in my tracks. The skin of the plant was a stark interplay between a deep, wet black and a white so pure that it was akin to an alabaster powder. The ebony and ivory were so slick and fathomless as to appear liquid. The colors were so well applied that it was nearly impossible to see where one ended and the other began. As such, I deemed it too beautiful to sever, so I instead planted my can spear headlong into the ground, and moved in for closer examination.

The vine was heavier than other vines, with a super substance to it, which felt wonderfully heavy and softly resistant. The stem had a fine grain to it, such as walnut burl, impossibly polished. Only upon running my hand in the opposing direction, could I detect the subtle resistance of any grain at all. The whole of that vine was something of a dream. And then, it wasn't.

As I was studying the vine, holding the heft of it in my hands, I was taken aback by a pulse that ran suddenly through it. The feeling occurred so unexpectedly, that I thought I imagined it. And then, to ratify the initial throb, it undulated in my grasp again, retreating upward into the canopy, by way of the small circumference created by my inspecting hands! The movement of the plant sent my eyes searching skyward, following the bichromatic thread of it, which was in stark relief against the rest of the canopy.As if attempting to find the end of a tangled rope, I followed the curves faithfully, at last finding myself spun in a 180-degree aspect, my eyes having returned to the earth immediately behind me. There, at the height of my chest, was the massive, floating head of an Anaconda!

The beast's face was a terrifying frontage of the serpentine harlequin. The hovering head was positively breathtaking in scale, the shape of an exaggerating spade. As great a presence as the cranium cast, the creature's eyes were disproportionate still, setting at least a time and a half too large, retreating at soft, upward diagonals, until they each disappeared astern. The size of those eyes was amplified by depth, where cerulean pools dissolved by slow gradient into deep blue lagoons. I was so close to it, that for the first time since being lost in that vastness, I could see a muddled reflection of myself in the deep foreverness of those eyes; which reflection only served to remove any doubt that I was be-snaked.

The head was perfectly still, but I could feel the hypocrisy of the beast, as the remainder of its length worked with a fever through my then open hands. The creature was easily nine meters long and well over 200 kilos. Its mouth was colored with a razor of that slick black, so that its lips appeared as knives, which drew to symmetrical points, accented by the acute angles of its cheeks. Its tongue then began darting in and out, sampling the film of my chest repeatedly, with the force and scale of a baby's arm.

I was frozen, as I might have been at the wrong end of a gun. I thought to reach for my planted cane with stealth, in an effort to behead the thing, but the congestion of our positions and the superior speed of the snake, left me to think myself better to remain still. Foolish.

It was then I felt the very end of its length, reversing its direction, running backward through my hands. It was a wonder to be locked into the eyes of that freak, unable to move, and to know that its body was working wildly to secure itself about me. Somehow, the contradictory activities of its head and its stretch had served to retard my response, until, at last, I had been mesmerized into complete inertia.

Before I could say 'breathe', the creature's wagger had anchored itself inside the crease between the crest of my thigh and the trough of my groin. It then lashed the void between thighs, fastening me into a quickly woven sheep shank, upon which it began to build a full coil. Time did not simply rush, but evaporated, all that while I failed to act.

There I was, finally cocooned in the rope layers of that Anaconda, such that its full length had wrapped about me three and a half times. Entombed there, as it were, I could hear the muffled innards of the snake. The pulsing of its heart. The gurgling of its digestive tract. The slippery sound of writhing bonelessness. At last I was overcome, knowing that even one slight twitch from me and that snake would surely crush me in reflex. It was all I could do, betraying every instinct to fight, so that I could remain perfectly still.

My stillness was not a tactic born of courage, but from a lack of options. In the short term of my imprisonment, the approach had proved successful, as the beast had not yet crushed me, as well it could have done. An instinct in me then, nothing more than an instinct in me then, suggested that I extend my physical surrender completely to the force of the snake.

As if 'uncoiling' myself, I began subtly yielding my body, beginning at my crown and moving nether-ward through my full trunk. My capitulation was so deft, so silently done, that it was as if my surrender was a thief, which moved through the whole of me, never the least detected by that snake. At last, I had set every muscle in my body to simultaneous rest, my feet were no longer touching the earth, so that I was quite literally afloat, mid-snake.

In all of that process, the snake's head never moved, nor did its eyes even once turn themselves askance of me. It was a fat irony: my total relaxation in the very grip of death itself. All ambition foreclosed upon and replaced by a cascading waterfall of willingness; a willingness to live...to wait...to sleep...to die.

The time had come, and the Anaconda, in a great yawning gesture, unhinged its massive jaw. Its gape revealed a sarcastic pink tunnel, whose overt sweetness was betrayed by the dank rot of its deepest gut, which produced a stench akin to fetid tulip water.

At the fullest articulation of its neck, at the very end of its range, I heard a wild sound, which was as the crackling of cellophane or the rustling of a taught plastic. It was a thin, brittle, fracturing sound. My eyes then clapped shut and I waited to be et. And waited. And waited still.

To my surprise, the creature then closed its great mouth, still not constricting me as it could do. I forced my eyes open to the least degree possible, until I beheld a wonder, which caused them to saucer. When the mouth of the snake returned to the closed position, an amazing sight was produced, as the black and white greasepaint of skin covering that creature's sloped face was then peeling away. The exterior colors had been shattered, becoming a translucent skin, which looked as if it had been rolled back with a key, like a lid of sardines.

The full power of the snake's gaze repurchased me, only there was a profound change underway. Those formerly dark cerulean eyes had become as a kaleidoscope. It was as if the lenses of its eyes had been shattered with the skin of it, forming a broken pane through which it began to broadcast a ladder of colors. The colors began in a family of reds, moving through a field of oranges, greens and blues. As the sequence was completed, the last radiant color of that magnificent amethyst; a limpid, aniline purple.

The creature then began an unhurried process of dis-coil, its head making stretched passage first. I was frozen in the rope of the thing, as its head disappeared from my outlook, followed by its full, undulating taper. My spear was still plonk heavily in the adjacent earth, providing just the sheer type of edge to assist the beast in the massive project of shedding!

The snake's emergence from the slough was done with such competence of an orange peeled in an unbroken skein, leaving the skin behind in full tact. I was left awash in the opaque sleeve, swimming in a black and white, empty stocking.

Unexpectedly, unbelievably free, I swiveled to watch the snake make passage to the basal exit at the end of the corridor. No longer that malevolent black and white monster, the skin of it had been completely forfeited, leaving it: a magnificent and inching golden thread. Its flaxen glow illuminated the interior of the passage around it, until the dark tunnel had become a beautifully lit cocoon. At last, the snake disappeared through the opening, leaving me to loose myself from that colossal dermis.

I grabbed my steadfast spear, wondering bewildered to the end of the downward corridor to gaze out its end, at last...

CHAPTER 12

GOD'S POCKET

raced to the tunnel's end, but to my great misfortune, my feet were unable to keep up with the rest of me, resulting in my taking a nasty spill, which sent me headlong into the earth. The slickness of the jungle floor AND the steepening downhill grade, facilitated an uncontrolled belly slide toward the opening at the end. As I was gaining undesired speed and approaching the hatch, I discovered the termination facing me was a very steep drop... which realization appeared to have come too late for remedy.

While sliding, I was stretching wildly with all four of my limbs, panicked to find some anchor to which I could fix myself, as a way of slowing my onrushing destruction. I briefly caught a low tangle with my right hand, but when the vine snapped under the weight and velocity, I merely aggravated my speed with spin, until I found myself in a full, flat spiral. Any resultant slowing was not nearly enough, so as I was being hurtled over the precipice, all I could do was make one last blind stretch. My splayed fingers set forth in ten unique arrays, resulting in the index and middle finger of my left hand, finding a small purchase 'round an erstwhile manzanita root, which was itself orphaned, outstretched from the cliff. After a few moments, I came to a final rest, as a waning pendulum or better yet, the wagging tongue on the face of that cliff. Hanging at a true six o'clock, I was suspended by one uncertain root, arms extended vom tag, trapped against the wall of that jungle fjord over two hundred meters above the earth. Prostrate there, I looked downward to find my free falling spear was finishing its sheer descent, plonking itself on end in the soft jungle floor.

I knew that a good plan right away was better than a perfect plan later, as I would need the full strength of my arms, which were already weakening by the passing seconds. Adjacent to my longitude, about five meters port, there was a motley shrub growing unkempt from the cliff. It was nearly classifiable as a small tree and it looked to have substance enough to support my weight, providing the promise of a rung allowing access back to the plateau just above. That was the argument FOR attempting to access the plant. A quick survey of other options came up nil, so that it became the only argument of any kind.

The best chance was to re-initiate a pendulum swing upon the root, so that a centripetal force might deliver enough throw to toss me to the adjacent mangle. As I swung, I prayed, gaining momentum by slow degree. I could, however, hear the root hairs at the center of that braid, giving way, fraying one thread at a time. The greatest force of weight on the root, of course, was when I swung through the bottom of the arc, so that each time I moved through that six o'clock position, I did so with an impossibly clenched bung. At last, I released, as an acrobat, landing with force in the shrub, distributed like a rag doll...but alive! Finding a quick footing, I was able to scale again to the relative safety of the elevation above.

The mix of gratitude, relief and exhaustion sent me to my knees, the posture of a penitent savage, my face falling into my open hands. I admit I wept, uncontrollably. Weeping had to have been the only way of releasing all of that tension AND to metabolize the dosage of adrenaline, which had me in a full body tremor. After a time, I regained my composure, and I finally lifted my face from my hands, to survey the site.

From the look of it, I had emerged from a natural drain pipe in the bush. The space I occupied there was the equivalent of a forest balcony, allowing only two or three steps laterally, offering no other escape. Looking back upward, into the pipe from which I had come, the ground was far too slick and the grade too steep for a simple return from whence I came. For the moment, no escape appeared possible and so I simply sat, quite still, in the forest mezzanine, and, I suppose, I let go.

To this day, I am still astounded, that at that worst moment, I beheld the single most beautiful vision I have ever seen. A moment like that is one for which the word 'sublime' was created. Only sublime simultaneously captures the presence of 'beauty wrapped in terror'. Sublimity what I was about to behold from that dizzying veranda.

As I raised my face, I was greeted by a high and moonlit view of a never ending jungle far, far beneath me. From my position, I was sharing the perspective of God's highest creatures, so that the fronds and leaflets, the bracts, the blades, were all beneath me—like an undulating carpet, which extended into the foreverness of that Amazonian horizon.

The sky above me was equally magnificent, where I was attended by a blond and crescent moon, which had been hammocked in the cobalt. The moon was as a celestial street lamp, casting a pale-blue gauze over the world below, and deepening the amplitude of every color in its sweep.

I can say, without reservation, that in my lifetime, that was the truest view of heaven I ever saw; perched there as I was, with a view of that blue-black night, dusted by that river of stars, which had been scattered above me, as if they were diamonds that had fallen from a hole in God's pocket.

Soft as it was, even that moonlight was enough to briefly glaze my retinae, the result of all that time spent in the darkness of the canopy and that tunnel of horror. As my eyes resisted arrest, a clarity of focus in the nearer distance delivered the view of a discordant intrusion amidst that swelling Arcadia.

The distant canopy of the jungle was unbroken in every direction, which only served to make more stark, a fierce and ragged opening which appeared in a tree bluff just below me. Into the density of forest, a great depression had been torn, such as might have been made by the foot of a passing giant. The whole of that detrusion created an amphitheater, at the center of which appeared the remains of a downed craft.

CHAPTER 13

SPELUNKING

pon sight of that plane, the promise of fellow humanity brought my focus to a keen point. Need gave birth to Invention, and, as is so often the case, the solution to my problem was wrapped within the very problem itself. After all, there is no direction that I could look, no step that I had taken, without encountering some form of leviathine vine, which fell, without fail, from the highest of that canopy to lowest of the forest floor.

I began immediately, collecting a fat vine, spooling the length of it upon my porch, in the discipline of sailor stacking the halyard of a mainsail. The weight of it and the time it took, left me with a cramping back, the muscles in which came to feel as a writhing bag of snakes. After fifteen minutes, I arrived at the cable's end, which must have constituted at least 150 meters of line. With the fluency of a ship's captain, which I might well have been, for all I knew at the time, I fashioned a bowline about my waist, as a makeshift safety harness, all the while, praying it would never come in handy.

Spelunking. That is a rather nasty sounding word for repelling into an abyss, for the word smuggles within itself, the very sound of a soft object crashing to earth with a great 'splat'. Quite the opposite of what one hopes to experience while climbing, but, the perfect word for me at that time. The worst of the challenge, as you might imagine, was the initial leaning out over the ledge, knowing that my only separation from a free fall into the void, was the strength of those untested vines and the quality of my knot. Very few moments in life are as pure as those, where the fullness of one's focus is reduced to such a tight point of singularity. I grabbed a third vine, for good measure.

Peering over the face of the cliff, I looked down and was braced by the blast of a rising thermal, which blew my hair back and roared about my ears, amplifying the dizzy height. The wind made for an excellent accomplice to the mushrooming darkness, feeding my imagination, so that at last I looked down into that sweltering, convinced that I was about to descend into the throat of a waiting behemoth. Additionally, the verticality of the cliff was so extreme that it appeared to retreat inward beneath me, so that it was not merely vertical, but invertical.

Upon that night sky, the actual floor at the bottom was not visible, appearing only as a gnarl of darkness at the bottom of a well. Grabbing three vines for all they were worth, I eased my way over the edge of that cliff, so that I was suspended those hundreds of meters above the floor. With all the speed of a sloth, I inched down the jungle pigtails.

I was past the point of no return, perhaps fifty meters down the vine, when my palms were drenched with perspiration, which made the grainless vines nearly impossible to hold on to. To compensate, my groin acted as an incompetent vice, so that before long my legs were shuddering and my biceps and shoulders were alight with a thin glaze of fire. One hundred meters down. Half way, I guessed. I would not make the full distance; I knew it then. There are such moments in life where one can't let go until one can't hold on. With that observation, the thenars of both palms began to seize, resulting in my involuntary release of those cables. It was the work of my clenched legs alone then, which would slow my decent, but with the gaining of speed, the loin cloth provided no protection, so that my gonads were being rapped like a speedbag by those thousands of tiny buds, which acted as miniature knuckles for the length of that vine. It was over...I released completely...freefalling.

I fell...and fell...and fell into the darkness. I was face up, falling like a halibut through space, eyes heavenward. Time slowed, as is rumored to in the moments before death, but given that I was under the spell of amnesia, I had no inventory of life to flash before me. So, there was only my full attention on the falling, until—

I could hear a whipping sound, as a lasso being spun above my head! The bowline! The leafy harness about my waist was the only chance left, as I approached the earth past terminal velocity. My eyes could see the length of vine unspooling from the high perch, until the last of it was deployed. I was supremely confident that I would be snapped in two, with the seizing of that line, delivering me to an alternative form of death.

The line, however, proved of great elasticity, stretching and slowing my fall...stretching...stretching. I could hear the sound of ferocious snapping and writhing and cracking of that vine far above me. My fall was slowing, but not stopping. As I got near the bottom, I could at last see the approaching deck! My slowing would not prove enough, I was certain, as the floor was within ten...seven...five...meters...and then it snapped!

I landed on my back, in a teeming of soft vines and grasses, the wind emptied completely from me. With the force of the crash, I could feel all of the magma in me surging to my head, and with no crater from which I could erupt, my eyes fished outward, bulging wildly from their sockets. As I rolled about the primeval forest floorin agony, recovering my breath and vision, I discovered just an arm's length to my right, my trusted cane, planted at full attention, waiting for its master...

CHAPTER 14

REMAINS

he changing of the guards in heaven was well under way, as I arrived to the edge of the clearing, within shouting distance of that plane. As the aubade of morning announced the sky, the moon was not given the luxury of descent, instead, bullied by the fat fingers of dawn, it merely opaqued.

Upon sight of that craft in the meadow's midst, my heart grew wild, with the promise of some fellow traveler in the jungle morass. I was but several strides into the clearing, when I was arrested by a familiar scent. I quietly drifted to one knee, so that the waist high grasses of the meadow, tipped just at the level of my eyes. My nose, then the competent biographer of breezes, interpreted the draft as the one and only piquant of the cat. His zest hung low in the meadow, though it was dappled with intermittent breezes and competing fragrances in the pasture. At last, each peppered pulse of that essence collected, until it became the incomparable, windswept signature of the beast.

My ears set back at forty fives, the tips elongating to dull points, as a duet of German soldiers, shouldering their rifles. While the cat was no place to be seen, it was certainly him, as his specific musk had formed a keloid upon my very soul. As the scent of him paled with the moon, I surmised the beast nocturnal, and as such, assumed him to have been dissolved by the dawn.

There upon one knee, my senses then toggled, so that my sight was fully deployed upon the meadow. I would discover, that more curious than that great rent in the jungle's canopy, which could be explained by the crash, was the dull and dominant color of a beige—nature's unique stamp upon half-life. Unlike the vitality of the world I had known that far, the prairie was a study in atrophy, where the absence of water and the punishment of light, worked together to form a wasteland there.

As I rose to survey the plane itself, I discovered it to be entangled in a complex network of fossilized branches, such that it looked to be in the clutches of dead man's fingers. Each step forth to the plane, revealed that even the earth itself had been blighted, until it was literally charred immediately around the craft itself. Standing at the epicenter, looking outward to the rich perimeter of jungle, I could appreciate the macabre counterpoint of that site to the rest of creation...it was a study in comprehensive death.

I was calling out to an unlikely anyone whom I might be approaching. "Halloo," I yelled. "Halloo...?" My calling was to no affect from my position and so I made the few meters journey to close the complete distance, then standing just beside the plane. Upon my fix, so close to it, a very strange affect was at work over my full form. With every advancing step, I had experienced a pronounced tickling across my flesh, which eventually rose to the feeling of my being an easement for an army of ants. Initially, my flesh merely goosed, but eventually, when I was within a few meters of the wreckage, every hair upon the length of me was standing fully erect. Whether the adrenaline, the fear or the fierce static charge, the result was that I looked the muted version of a porcupine.

The plane itself was of the smaller variety of craft, featuring propellers and wings mounted in the low position to an elongated fuselage. The useful load of it could not have translated to more than eight passengers at once, I concluded. The look of it gave evidence that it had been long resting there, as oxidization and rust had been at hard work across the skin of it, gnawing their progress, as soldiers in a jagged forward area.

Where the aft cabin doors should have been located, a permanent opening had been made, as those doors had been long collapsed from their jamb. The calcified portal was enrapt by complex arteries of petrified growth, which served to overstate the haunt of the place. The adjacent wings and mutilated propellers were beyond repair, were there a living soul who might have done.

BINGE

My keener inspection delivered me to a much more queer observation with respect to that plane's body. The metal skin of the fuselage was quite rigorously covered in hatch marks, which were serving to tally sets of five. The scoring of those sets was in the traditional format of four upright marks diagonaled by single line. The tallies had been recorded in black wax, which was, it seemed, the work of a child's crayon. By my rough calculation, there were thousands of those hatchings.

The hair of me had then become as wire, as I determined to hoist myself up through the ragged opening just behind the plane's hips. As my fingers wrapped themselves about the inside of the frame, in preparation for leveraged ascent, the hairs upon my arms began falling out, as if the petals of a dying flower. I immediately removed my hands in horror and the shedding stopped. Upon returning my balding grasp to the plane, my deciduous forearms became completely bare.

I breached the gape, such that the weight of me caused the ancient craft to creak and heave port, toward me. Once inside the plane itself, I wrestled with some difficulty to find a center-line, which would stabilize the rocking of the thing. At last, the interior came to rest at a soft, but permanent angle. The whole of that plane was cocked to the left, as the wing of that side had been snapped, and the fuselage consequently crank.

At first glance, the plane was long emptied of passengers, but was littered in exploded luggage and other non-human cargo. There was, however, a warning fist, which met me there, as the ambient was infused with the brewing smell of rut, which indicated something organic had been at long decay therein.

As I stood, hunched by the short, parabolic ceiling, I was startled find that my Saint Christopher medallion had met me half way, floating in mid-air before me. Had it not been tethered to the chain, it should have fulfilled its ambition, fastening itself to the ceiling. It was then I became aware that the walls of the plane were strewn with metal objects, like shells cast upon a magnetic shore. Seat belts, forks, pens and even ashtrays that once recessed in the arms of the passenger seats, all stuck to the interior walls and ceilings. The collage of metals was further amplified by the arithmetic wall paper of tick marks, such that the ones covering the exterior of the plane, counting those sets of five.

My eyes, at last, arrived the short distance to the cockpit, where they discovered what they craved least. There, snapped at an obtuse angle to the femur, was the lower leg of someone in the pilot's seat. "Halloo? I am not here to harm you." I entered, cane spear first, "I am coming in, now. Halloo." There was no response, sending a chill through me, as I sensed the presence of Death. I wiped the panic from my forehead, only to discover that the back of my hand was then littered with the forfeited brow of my eye.

I entered the tiny cabin to discover the remains of the pilot. He was frozen in his character, the affects, I supposed, of rigor mortis. His face was a bloodless granite, though his dark aviator glasses gave him the quality of merely seeming dead. He was really quite dignified, sitting there at the helm, his dignity aided by the full pilot regalia, chevroned shoulders… gold wings at his breast. If I hadn't known better, I should have thought he was not a man at all, but a magnificent figure made of wax.

There was, however, the troubling incongruence between his being long dead AND the nearly perfect preservation of his flesh. Surely, thought I, a man so long expired, and based upon the age of the crash site, very long expired, should have been reduced to bone by then.

The dread of being the presence of death had plumed to fill the frame of me, but given my lack of options, I simply could not risk the possibility that I had misdiagnosed him. Intimate and ghoulish as it was, I sought final confirmation by searching the pulse at his decrepit neck. When my fingers came to even the lightest initial contact with his skin, I found the flesh there was but a veil of rice paper, so thin that my touch broke the surface. I jumped back in horror, but the puncture created no release of fluids, indicating, he was in fact, long deceased.

Deeply shaken, I turned my attention away from the corpse, scanning the cockpit for any other hope. I found the silenced radio, which I worked with a fever to raise for outside contact. In the end, it was as much a fool's errand as praying that the pilot had been the least bit living. Desperate, amidst all that promise in that plane, my desperation was being mocked, so that my heart finally cratered. I had so fallen for the false promise of human contact, through that pilot, the radio or otherwise. Ultimately, I was only surrounded by brokenness.

As the sun rose to a more prominent position in the sky, above the bluff of trees around the place, a flood of white light entered the cockpit focused to a sharp point by the windshield of the plane. That burst of light was so sudden and severe that I was temporarily blinded. I shuttered my eyes as quickly as I was able, not at all confident that I had responded in time. The only promise I had was in the kaleidoscope of colors floating about the interior darkness behind my clinched lids. The light was so bright that it proved an acid in my eyes, melting the deep film therein, so that it felt like hot oil running down the interior wall at the back of my skull.

And then, in the deep pitch of ocular dystrophy, my bowels were turned to water as I heard a raspy voice behind me, "Esau... Esau...is that you?"

I turned slowly to face the voice, through the cage of my desperate fingers and melting eyes. It took several moments to recover the smallest fraction of my sight, which delivered the dim, unfocused view of the pilot, alive!

BINGE

CHAPTER 15

PILOT EPISODE

 was riveted into the co-pilot's seat in terror, then face to face with a zombie! The pilot was a combination of physical death and, yet, the life that was there within him. Nothing on earth could be thus, thought I.

My eyes deliquesced almost completely, more liquid than solid, continued melting as the great star took its full position above the treeline. I did what I could do to remain fastened upon the man, but the horrifying view of him and the brilliance of that light created a visual agony.

"That radio, Esau, it won't work here." The man spoke to me in a conversational tone, as if he had not been dead moments earlier AND as if he knew me. Neither of which was possible.

Terrified as I was, his view of me must have been equally horrifying, as I was a violent looking savage, holding a spear and trying desperately to steal his radio. I choked out, "S-s-sir..? I mean you no harm."

He was unmoved by my mania, "I knew you would survive. And here you are, my Esau."

He was clearly in bottom of death's spiral, which had, I suspected, fed his delusion. I could only think to respond, "You look to be in such pain, sir. What can I do to help you?"

"Yours is not to worry for me, Esau. I am as I am. Beyond the wish of relief, except that which is final."

His insistence on my identity, it seem to me, cruel to play along with him. I could not bear to be the last lie in the life of a dying man...a suffering man. So, I lumpishly offered, "I'm so sorry, sir, but I am not who you think I am, this Esau. I am a man...as lost in this jungle as you are, I fear."

Nonplussed, the corners of his mouth appeared to dawn with an attitude of... of pride, really. "You are my son. You are much older now, but even a dying father can still sense the presence of his own child. Come here. Come closer to me, my Esau. I will show you."

The pilot light of terror was then ignited to full flame, such that the impulse was screaming in me to run from the place. Only upon recalling it now, in the calm condition of retrospect, do I know why I didn't run, when all reason dictated that I should do. It was one thing, and one thing alone, that nailed me there. It was the image of such suffering. It was not reason or strength or character. It was compassion alone, which emerged in me, as the involuntarily reaction. I was both terrified and sorrow-filled with the proximity of such comprehensive suffering in a stranger. Fastened to that spot, I responded, "I cannot move, sir. I have become nearly blind by this light, which is pouring upon us now. It is much, much too bright. I can't see the way to you."

"Has the sun come up, then?" he asked, making no sense at all.

"Can you not see it, sir, the sun?" I asked, in disbelief.

"Esau, I am blind. Come, take my glasses, boy. Take them from me."

While there was the fear of him again trying to get close to me, for God knew what evil purpose, I could not open my eyes without some form of protection. So, I reached out cautiously and began to remove the glasses. The glasses were attached to his face, that the skin of his temples had welded around the stems.

"Just take them off, Esau. You won't hurt me." he gently instructed.

With that, I peeled them away, both the glasses and some layers of flesh with them. He did not bleed.

He spoke to me, in the manner of comforting, "I know that you are afraid. Don't be afraid of me. I am not in pain anymore."

I put the aviators on, which brought immediately relief, but also a real clarity of vision, which revealed the horror of details in that pilot's face. In the dim view of him before full sunrise, he looked the perfect wax figure, a trick of strategic shadow. In the full and unforgiving light pouring through the windshield, he was anything but vital. He was gaunt to the point of skeletal, all the muscle and fat long dissolved away from the bone, leaving his face to look like a thin sack filled with broken glass. As if it were not enough, the structure of that horrified face, the skin over the whole of him, from his long thin neck to his balded crown, was covered in chronic wounds. Those wounds were, no doubt, the result of an ongoing disagreement between the underlying bone and his wizened skin. His eyes, then in full view to me, were in deep retreat, glazed with the unhomogenized milk, which cloaks the eyes of the blind.

"Is that better for you, my son?" he offered knowingly.

Swallowing my revulsion, "Yes, sir. Thank you."

BINGE

"You see now, I have no need of them. They are your inheritance. Come now, kneel here where I can reach you."

My compassion was surely tested, as I did move closer to him, finally kneeling in the cove that was formed between his snapped right leg and his opposite knee. He raised his hands blindly, brailing his way around my waiting face. His fingers were brittle and gnarled with the atrophy...of death. With the touch of death upon my face, a deep chill was alight the full length of me.

He spoke as his fingers travelled, "You see, my Esau, he has a deep, crescent scar..." He brailed his way about my face, to gain his bearings, finally reaching beneath the stem of my glasses, to the corner of my eye. "This scar, it extends from the corner of his left eye..." His ancient fingertips dwelt there, following a deep signature from the corner of that eye and down-cheek. "...to the head of his jaw." His face registered confirmation, as he concluded, "You are my son. You see, even a blind man, knows the presence of his own child."

He then reached out and took my wrist, guiding my hand to the scar, running my finger through it. It was true! There was a crescent scar!

"How? How could you know this?! How can this be?!" I exclaimed. A scrum arose in me between total disbelief, abject terror and dawning hope. "Sir, please tell me,,, tell me who am I?"

"Esau, there is no time. I have no time, now that you have come. Your brother will tell you what you need to know. Your brother, he is all that matters now. Do you understand me?"

I was a in a stunned silence, failing to respond. The pilot was breathing with increased difficulty. He was waning, to be sure. Using whatever breath he could muster, he communicated with an urgency.

"Esau, I know that you are lost and afraid. Don't be afraid for me. Your brother, Jacob. You must protect Jacob. Promise me."

He was nearly gone, his last few breaths then in the shallows.

"Yes. Yes, sir. I promise."

He raised a clumsy right hand, searching for the top of my head, finally resting them there.

"Esau, I have always loved you. You must know that, if nothing else. I might have done better for you, had I known... better...but, I did what I could do. You are always my boy. Protect your brother...my Esau...."

His last sigh carried upon it, this name. The breath left him permanently, as he died right before my eyes. As his dead hand

BINGE

fell from the top of my head, the rigid fingers took with them a fist of my hair, which was falling from me in tufts.

Tears ran from my eyes like a river, I screamed in a rage to the heavens, "What the fuuuuuuuuuuuuuck??????!!!!! God, what is this hell that you have put me in?!!!!!!!!"

I was in a full tantrum, shaking the dead pilot and throwing my fists about the cockpit in a rage! I tore the useless radio and threw it to the ground, where I began jumping up and down on it, until it was rubble! Tearing away at the seats and smashing anything that would break, including a long mirror running the length of the above the windshield.

As I looked into that shattered mirror, my reflection was faceted in a hundred shards, so that I could only see myself in pieces, as if I was a puzzle exploded. Peering into that glass, I could fit only enough to see the scar extending from my left eye, which was deep and pronounced. I further could see that my head was completely bald and my face was alight in that blood and sweat and filth, which had come to cover me in the jungle.

Exhausted, I fell to my knees, face in my crazed hands, once again. In that comprehensive despair and that tide of silence which rose about me, I heard a whirring sound. I could not bear to open my eyes and face the insistent and discordant sound, which was approaching me. The sound was something like a coin, spinning slowly on a table, surrendering its velocity to gravity...

I splayed my fingers, looking up the aisle to the cabin of that plane, to find an object on the ground, rolling toward me, until it finally met the dam of my praying knees.

It was an orange crayon...

STOWAWAY

here was no negotiating the rustling sound at the back of the plane. I had heard it. The surest evidence of its being real was my desperation to un-hear it. My mind was a cracker, crumbling for a failure to metabolize any more of the madness in that place. My heart had taken cover somewhere in my bowels, as I again was forced to face the waiting peril, just five meters aft my position.

I was holding the crayon in my right hand fingers and the trusted spear in my dominant left. As I summoned my full focus, my mind was at high treason, unwilling to let go the tiny detail of that crayon in my fingers being orange, while all the marks about the plane were black. Of what importance could that possibly be, thought I, given the more than fifty incidents of insanity that I had faced, since discovering that I had been buried alive?!

I raised the spear before me, carrying it in the manner of a knight's lance, moving reluctantly though the insufficient height of that plane, until I arrived three paces from the tail.

"I know someone is there. I mean you no harm, friend. I come in peace." The calm and command of my voice was counterfeit, as my taught emotional state, was such that I was sure I would shatter, should anything, but a cricket emerge from the back of the plane. "I am armed, I warned. I am a savage and will give no thought to slitting your throat where you stand. You have this moment to reveal yourself with no harm to come."

The back of the plane remained perfectly still. The interior of the plane was akin to a war-torn building, where age had ravaged the fixtures and the crash has distributed the stowage erratically about the place. I suppose that is what made the rather intentional organization of blankets and boxes at the back left corner of the plane, so conspicuous. Order where there should have been chaos.

As I stared at the civilized heap, I was convinced that my fear was causing my mind to animate the pile, so that it looked to be rising and falling. After a moment of stillness, it was clear that there was dim movement in the hoard, so that it appeared as if it were shallowly...breathing.

Spear rising to my shoulder's height, I shouted filled with fear of my own, "I know that you are there and I will kill you, I promise." No response came, but my unease was ratified, when I caught sight of dull, pearly glint. I tamed the blurriness from my vision, which produced the clear definition of a white ball, that of an eye, peering through a slot in the jumble. With the tip of my spear, I began peeling away at layers of blankets, as leaves from a woven artichoke, until, at last, I came to the heart of it: the terrified and tortured face of a small boy.

He was pulled together in a kinder-knot, his arms wrapped securely about his knees, which were pulled as tightly as they could be, to his chest. Looking upon his tiny crown, he was nearly Rastafarian, were the dreads upon his head so locked in filth. His eyes were tightly clenched and he was fiercely trembling, as a boy awaiting his execution. I was shocked, standing over him, not certain how to digest the sight, for all that I had considered to be hiding there, I had not considered him.

My shocked silence lasted long enough that the boy's eyes began to blink into the reluctant status of open. He stared up at me, in his terror, revealing an impossibly dirty face, haunted by years of wear far past his own. Our eyes met and he surely saw in me the demon savage, who he thought had come to slay him dead, where he sat. I tried to urgently put him at ease, "Oh, oh small boy..." said I, "...don't fear. I won't hurt you."

Without warning and in an instant so fast as to be unmeasurable, he sprung, leaping at me, all four limbs outstretched, until he octopussed himself around the whole of me. I was as be-child then, as I had been be-snake before!

He cried out, "I was so scared! But I knew you wouldn't lie to me! I knew you'd come! I never doubted, Esau!"

From my muffled position, buried in the starfish he had assumed, I knew that I had no recollection of that child in my life AND that his strength was magnificently disproportionate to his diminutive scale. There, in my smothered position, I could hear his tiny heart beating wildly in his chest and the shaking of his body vibrating all around me. There, too, was the issue of my own heart, which had stopped beating briefly, which I was trying earnestly to start again. "There, there, it's alright, now." I comforted. "I've got you. I've got you. Be still, now. You're safe now."

With that, he finally relaxed his great hold on me, so that I was hefting him in the right angle of my bent left arm, in the manner that one holds a child much smaller. Looking into his eyes, I asked gently, "Will you be alright, now, if I put you down?"

BINGE

CHAPTER 17

THE PARACHUTE

e stood before me, looking as much a nest built by careless birds, as he did a boy. He stood all of an awkward meter and a half. He was so impossibly thin, that the weight created by that mop of his hair, looked to threaten the stem of him. He wore thick eyeglasses, which bore the evidence of such damage as might have come from a year beneath the wheels of a tank. His clothing, could it really have been called such, was threadbare and ripe, dissolving into mere rags. His pants, the worst of it, were but a short mantle, fastened to him, I suspected, by a layer of filth, which had congealed to a tack.

It was those pants, which created the distressing view to a litany of gashes, which had been visited upon his legs. The varying freshness of his wounds, indicated that his legs were being cut to ribbons on some cadence, which I thought to be regular. Some lacerations were long since healed to become great longitudinal

THE PARACHUTE 99

scars, resting as a dim purple stripes beneath the milky surface of his skin. Still others had only recently scabbed over, fragile enough, certainly, to recur with even the slightest brushing of them. But worst of all and most prominent among them, was the layer so fresh that it was still seeping with the reactive surge of fluids from inside him. Something in the expression of my face and the intensity of my focus upon him, caused him to withdraw the spectacle of those legs from my view. The physical expression of his shame and self-consciousness.

"What has happened to your legs, boy?" I asked.

He was non-responsive and so, I asked again, "I say, you look like you've really hurt yourself there. Your legs. How did that happen?"

"I don't wanna talk about it." he sheepishly answered. He was clearly distressed, hiding his face from me, and so I gave wide berth from further interrogation. As he turned from me, however, and even stranger article was revealed upon his back. He was wearing a substantial pack, which was akin to a child's backpack, only massively more complex and much too large for him.

"I'll tell you what. I won't ask about those cuts on your legs again, if you'll answer a different question for me, okay?"

He turned and faced me again, clearly relieved of my letting go the topic of those wounds. "What is that you have strapped to your back?"

He looked reluctant to answer, until his expression finally melted with his response, "You're not still mad about it, are you?"

"Mad? Still?" "Why would I be mad?"

"I tricked you. You told me that I'd better not be lying, but then I was lying."

"I'm so confused, that's all. I'm not mad at you. Why would you think that?" I asked. He shrugged his little shoulders. "Just tell me, what is that pack for?"

"The parachute." His voice was tinted with the reluctance of a confession, which was nearly as interesting to me, as the answer itself.

"You had that parachute when this plane crashed?"

"You already know. We all did. Except Daddy. Why are you pretending, Esau?"

He was sincerely agitated by my questioning, but his answers only created more confusion for me.

"I promise you, I'm not pretending. I just don't remember. I can't remember."

"That isn't true. How could you forget a plane crashing?"

"Well, that's a good question. Do you know what amnesia is?"

"When you can't remember something?"

"That's right. Well, I have amnesia, you see. Only, I didn't forget just something. I have forgotten...everything."

His expression was a mix of horror and concern. If what he was asserting was true, it must have been a terrible shock to think that he was, essentially, alone again.

"Oh, it's nothing to be afraid about. I know that I will get my memories back, because you will help me. Okay?"

He nodded, suspiciously.

"Now, I need you to tell me what happened, so I can start to remember. If you had a parachute, why didn't you jump? Were you afraid?"

"I wasn't afraid." he said sternly. "I could have jumped if I wanted."

"But, you didn't. You might have died in this crash, but you didn't jump. Why?"

"Daddy."

"Your dad told you not to jump?"

"No. Daddy didn't have a parachute. He was the only one, so I had to stay with my dad."

"That was very brave of you. You must really love your daddy, then."

He didn't respond, other than to look even more concerned at my not remembering anything. "Can you tell me where your daddy is now?" He looked at me, incredulous. "I know this is strange for you, but you promised to help me. Can you tell me where your daddy is now?"

Without taking his eyes from mine, he raised his arm, extending a finger and pointing to the cockpit...at the dead pilot sitting therein.

"The pilot? He's was your dad?"

"Don't say that! Don't ever say that!" he angrily responded.

"What? What did I say?"

"You said was! Don't ever say that again!"

Oh, fuck, I thought. The boy had no idea that the man was dead. Of all the cosmic cruelty in history, distilled to one fucking moment, that was surely it. I had arrived to that scene in just the seconds to become the messenger to that poor boy's orphaning. As if I was sneaking upon a deer in the woods, I knew that one false step from me, and the boy would scatter.

"I'm sorry for what I said about your dad. Okay?"

My apology only served to madden him even more. "Stop it! Stop it! Stop it, Esau!"

"What did I do now, boy?!"

"He's our dad! Our dad! Our dad! Stop lying! Why are you being this way?!" His anger was the dynamite, which burst the dam of emotions in him, so that a rain of fierce tears began. He was so consumed, as to be inconsolable. Nothing left that I could say, so I simply got down on my knees and brought him into my embrace.

"It's okay. It's okay. You're safe now. I am here. I will never let anything happen to you." My comforting only brought more tears to his eyes, and so he spent some great time buried in my shoulder.

Through his waning sobs, he cried, "Esau, I don't want you to have an amnesia!"

"There's a good lad." I coached. "We must be strong together, you and me. Can we do that, together?"

His inventory of tears was finally spent and he raised his face to me again. The flood of his sadness and fear and loss, had begun the work of cleansing the filth from his cheeks, which tears carried the silt downward to his delicate jaw, where it settled to become delta built of sorrow.

I looked him committedly in the eyes and said, "I am Esau, from now on. Okay? Esau. I can't believe that I didn't ask you your name. Nothing is more important to me than your name. If I am Esau, then who are you?"

"I am your brother, Jacob."

BINGE

CHAPTER 18

THE MIRROR

acob, indeed. Of course, he was the Jacob, to whom the pilot referred in his dying breath, as my brother. The Jacob whose ward I had committed to become in my promise to the pilot, as the breath of him vanished from his very chest. My mind was so turned inside out, that regardless the absurdity of circumstance, I resolved myself to believe, tipped by the thought that I should have been happier to be wrong and companioned, than to have been right and alone again.

"You are Jacob, my brother. I know this to be true, while I know nothing else. If you say to me, Jacob, that something is true, I will never doubt you again. We are brothers, and brothers never lie to one another."

Relieved to be companioned himself, the boy's demeanor was immediately lighter, which was the first relief to the gloom of that place, since first I set foot therein. He was fixated upon Saint Christopher medallion, which was afloat between us, under the magnetic force of that cabin. He reached out and took the charm between his fingers, studying it closely. "Why are you wearing Muzzy's necklace?"

"Muzzy..?" Oh, good Christ, I thought, the old woman! The woman who was buried next to me. The woman I had unearthed too late. The woman long, long dead. But, who was she to the boy?

"You must remember her, Esau, if she gave you this. Grandmother?"

With each discovered branch upon my family tree, it appeared that I was to be pierced through the heart again, discovering that all had perished in my presence, some fault of mine, no doubt, but none mourned by me, for the failing in my recollection. I cobbled together the silhouette of the answer, so that I did not break the oath to him, only seconds after making it, "Yes, I remember her. Muzzy is...Muzzy is back at the clearing that I came from. This is her necklace, which I am wearing for good luck."

"Why is she not with you?" he innocently queried.

Again, scrambling to assemble a Swiss-cheesed truth, the holes of which were omissions, "She was not in shape enough to come with me through this jungle to find you."

"That's why she gave you her necklace, then."

"Why's that, do you say?"

"Saint Christopher is the patron saint of travelers. It's protected you, till you got here. Muzzy always wears that necklace when we travel."

Privately, a bastard thought ran through my mind, which was that considering her condition when I found her, I might be best to take it off.

"Alright, then. Look at how well you are doing to help me, Jacob. Muzzy is our grandmother. The pilot is our father. And, you and I are brothers."

"Twins." he said matter of factly, still studying the charm.

"Well, I wouldn't say that we are twins exactly, but I have hope to discover that I am brave like you." I said, adult-patronizing-child.

"We are twins. Jacob and Esau. You know, like the Bible. We were born at the same time, cause I was holding on to your heel when we came out. That's how come. We're mirror twins."

Just as the footing of hope was presented, it was dissolving as a passing breeze. The boy had clearly gone mad. I felt my blood begin to boil in the heat of frustration, with the suspicion that I was being lied to by him. It was all I could do to hold what sanity remained to me. I was willing to accept the impossibility of all the conditions that far, but this newest claim, should I have accepted it, would have forced me to forfeit everything else that he had said, as untrue.

"Twins? Jacob, I don't think we are twins. I am at least thirty years older than you are. I am a man and you are still a young boy. You see, how we are not twins?" I reprimanded severely. "Jacob, I cannot be your brother, if you don't tell me the truth. I need you to be honest with me, like we said before, so I can help you. I know you are a good boy, Jacob. Tell me the truth."

He was nonplussed, "You have been away for a long time and I have been here. We are twins. I promise." he said so sweetly and the need in me made him greater, the elasticity of my willingness to believe.

He presented his case, instructing me with love, as if I was the small child and he was the adult. "I can prove it. See..."

he said, indicating to my spear, "...you hold your spear in your left hand, but I hold things in my right hand. Opposite. Like a mirror, remember." He then reached up, pointing to the scar at my left eye, "You have a scar from your left eye..." he began, as he removed his battered eye glasses, "...and I have a scar from my right eye."

It was a fact that he had a scar, the perfect match to mine!

"Birthmarks, see? Muzzy says that we used to be attached there, when we were inside Mommy."

My mind was reeling with the dizziness of his proposition. It was something to do with his insistence in the insanity, which made me think that I was the one who had gone mad. It was impossible to hear...to believe...to think of such a thing! But, just then, as I had resolved myself to deny any merit to his claims, a spark shot suddenly through the void, which was my present mind. There, at the center of an empty cave in me, there was the suggestion of a tiny flame, dancing atop a candle in my recall, until I found myself uttering it aloud, "Jacob The Right Hearted...?"

"Yes! Esau, yes! That's me! That's me! You remembered!!!" He was ecstatic and I was stunned and confused, shaking my head in effort to grow the memory still.

"What does it mean? What does it mean, Jacob? Jacob the Right Hearted..?" I said, with a welling optimism for the discovery of that thread, even so small it was, which might retrieve the fabric of my recall.

The boy reached out to my right hand, placing it upon the left side of my chest. "You see, Esau, your heart is beating there. Do you feel it? Do you?"

Within a few moments of concentrated effort, I did feel my racing heart, which I expected I would do. The boy then drew excitedly closer to me and guided me down to one knee. He then leaned his slight chest up against me, putting my ear to the RIGHT SIDE of it, where I could hear his heart beating wildly directly below the surface. "Do you hear it, Esau? Do you hear my heart beating on the right side?"

I did! It was madness, but the boy was right hearted! "Jacob, I hear it, as surely as you tell me! It's beating there; there at the right! But, how can this be?!" I asked, tears of gratitude ascending from the well of me.

"Mirror twins. I told you." he said, as happy to have returned that splinter of my identity, as he was to know that I had recovered the most important part of him: the memory of who he was. I grabbed him, clasping him tightly to me, my fingers dug deeply into that rag that was his shirt, "Oh, my God, I remember. I remember you, Jacob, my brother. Oh, God...gentle boy. Little Jacob. My truest friend." I withdrew him and looked into his muddy face, "I don't know how, but you are true."

"Daddy told me. Daddy told me you would come back. And you did. You did come back."

That promise of memory, still residing someplace in me, was like the sight of land to a man long lost at sea. To have been so nearly drown in that fugue, it seemed such a cruelty that my first act was to explain the difficult truth to my brother, who deserved it least.

"Jacob. Jacob, I must now tell you something because I swore that I would never lie to you. I have to tell you something, but when I do, you must know that I will always protect you."

His joy was thawing quickly to fright, as well it should have done, at the sudden seriousness of my voice. "No, Esau. You're scaring me. Don't."

"We are brothers, Jacob, so what is true for you is true for me. Twins, right?" I paused to think how to word the thing, but there was no packing it soft enough to make gentler the truth of what I had to say. "Jacob, when I arrived here, to this place, I found our father first. I spoke to him for a few minutes, but then..." There was no way, but to just say it, "Jacob, our father died just before I found you. I'm so sorry." My gut was clenched taught in preparation for his certain wailing.

I was shocked, instead, that a grin come across his face and that he shook his head, as if I had said something completely foolish. "Esau, he'll wake up. He'll wake up when the moon comes out. You'll see."

Oh, the poor boy, thought I. His frayed mind had finally broken under the torture of the place. "No, Jacob. He won't. I know that it's hard to hear, but our father is dead. He has no pulse. He's is not breathing. Jacob, I'm so sorry."

The boy was staring to the cockpit, where that lower leg of the pilot was bent at that rich angle to the femur. A mist of sad vacancy came over his eyes and his voice forlorned, "No, Esau. He dies every day. Every day, Daddy dies."

He took the orange crayon from my hand and two short steps to the bulkhead, just behind the cockpit. Climbing up on his tip toes, he added a diagonaled, orange tick mark, completing a set of five. As I looked at the marks in that small area, they were all orange, in stark contrast to the black ones which had grafittied the rest of the plane. There, in the collection of orange marks, were six sets of five, for a total of thirty.

"Jacob, what are all of these marks you've made?"

"Days."

"Days? These are all days? What days?"

"That we've been here, daddy and me. Daddy showed me how. Daddy dies, then I make the mark."

Knowing the units being measured by that sea of hatch marks took the breath from my chest and set my mind to spinning, in the further impossibility of what I was hearing. "Jacob, there must be thousands of those marks. They are all black, except for these few orange ones." I was afraid to ask, but had to know, "What do these orange ones mean, then?"

"Years. Daddy showed me how."

"Thirty years, Jacob? Today?"

"Yes. Today. Ten thousand, nine hundred and fifty days. And, Esau will come back. Just like Daddy said."

I said, stunned, "..And every day...?"

"...He dies, Esau. Every day, he dies."

𝔅𝔦𝔫𝔤𝔢

CHAPTER 19

THE DAMASK

t proved difficult for me, adapting to the lunar cadence of the meadow. The way of the place was nocturnal for one reason alone: the sun. The great star was not merely severe upon the clearing, but antagonistic. Its great heft hung over the horizon, the heaving gut of fire, oppressing every living thing thereunder. Whether blinding it, scorching it or parching it, the sun was unrelenting upon that spot. Sans the cover of the jungle umbrella, all life was forced to shelter where it could find, for the entirety of day. For Jacob and me, it meant that we spent daylight inside the wreckage, with that dead pilot and all the rest of it, awaiting a salve of moonlight.

I tried in earnest, to get some rest, but the combination of that nocturnal ethos and the liters of adrenaline coursing through me, worked against any stillness of mind. Truth be told, I was just as happy to lay in my position at the tail of that plane, and watch over my brother as he slept.

The experience of aloneness had not occurred to me in any meaningful way, until I was no longer alone...until, the discovery of him. He had retrieved me from the unwitting solitary confinement in my own mind, where I had discovered myself behind enemy lines. Jacob was the purpose beyond myself, which galvanized me. Wanting to rescue him from the coffin of that crate, worked wonders in providing me the first peaceful moments I'd had, since surfacing from that shallow grave. And that peace brought with it the ability to simplify my salvation to answering just one simple question: what was true?

The topography of that earth was challenging, to be sure, filled with obstacles of both terrorists and terrain, but I found that it paled in significance to the profound mental oppression therein. As it was, the tiny reservoir of ideas and beliefs, upon which I had always drawn, proved no use at all. Worse than that, in most cases, my assumptions had only thwarted my progress. There was an inversion in the place, an encryption, for which I held no key.

Had I been given a choice of one instrument with which to negotiate my way, it certainly WOULD NOT have been a compass. As valuable as a compass may have been, the instrument only orients itself to a superficial truth, that of North. The truth I required was something much more profound than simple direction. My quest, presently, was to find an unchanging key, a primer, a single truth around which I could organize some mental framework. After a time, meditating upon the specific problems became a problem of its own, as my energies became like fingers pulling at a knot, only serving to make it tighter. And so, I happily surrendered again, to the calm which attended me, in the watching of my brother sleep. It was within that calm, quite by accident, I found that single truth I required.

There is no lie in the face of a sleeping child, for their sleep is not encumbered with broken promises or unmet need or unfulfilled longings. The wonder of a child at rest, is their full presence in it, rosy cheeked and sprawling, as if they are beneath a spell cast by a benevolent fairy. Only at sleep, when they are so still, the innocence in them rises to their sleeping faces, like layers of sweet cream. Jacob the Right Hearted, my brother, slept just so, and I watched him for a long while. After those hours, studying him there, his face damasked in that virtue, I was finally convinced that he was incapable of lying and that in my small brother, I was seeing the best of myself, impossible as those circumstances made it seem.

As with all I had discovered in that terrene, so too was the portrait of my sleeping brother, presented in a wreath of doom. The innocence and devotion and goodness of Jacob was all the more prominent, for he had discovered such a peaceful rest, where he preferred to sleep each day, in the lap of a dead man. As quickly as I had resolved Jacob as the Rosetta Stone, my confidence was undermined by the cadaverous insanity of him in the couch of that pilot.

As ever, I worked quickly to rebuild that scaffolding of hope about my mind, assuring myself that Jacob's claims made as much sense as any of it. His veracity would be proved soon enough, as he had so confidently assured me of the dead pilot's resurrection with the rising moon. That rickety skeleton of reason re-attending me, my focus then drifted from the boy to the world outside the plane, where the finished day was being varnished by dusk.

As the sun set, the great sailcloth of sky above our position was translating from the hot white of that unforgiving daylight, to the gradient relief of cyan, the signature of night's dawning. The sky most central above our position was the furthest from that waning sun, and so became a royal mast of Egyptian blue, which anchored a cambering spinnaker of colors across the heavens. I awestruckedly inventoried from that Egypt, high above us, through swaths of color, from the Celeste and Keppel, which drifted slowly down the belly of the sky, until they arrived, at last, to meet with the final dusting of Verdigris. As that plume of color rippled through the sky, it disappeared softly into God's fat palm, someplace unseen beneath the horizon...someplace far, far from me.

As her final curtsey to arriving night, a collection of orphaned stratus clouds were lit to the colors of fire, in the backdraft of that setting sun, until they were as embers of driftwood, floating upon the upended sea. At last, the wash of Egyptian blue spilled fully across the sky and each paler hue was dissolved to it, until the morrow.

The waxed moon then asserted itself as governor of the heavens...and the cockpit stirred.

CHAPTER 20

TWO FACED

acob descended the pilot's lap, with the fluidity of a dancer, which was, I assumed, the polish of thirty years. Emerging in one deft motion, he spiraled like smoke from that lap, one leg outstretched grande adage, and floated to the floor, landing softly à terre, finally separating from the corpse. It was beautiful to watch, that dance, not only for the grace of that single, cursived motion, but for the great courtesy that sustained it just so. To think, how delicately the boy worked to preserve the sleep of a dead man.

As Jacob made his way from the cockpit, he wound through floating columns of shadow that hovered mid-air between us, drifting en avant toward me. The continued light elegance of his movement was in mute contrast to the dimness in his general character, especially about the face. In that new proximity, the details in his expression were illuminated by the moonlight, which made clear his waxiness. His face was expressionless, which served to exaggerate a great openness of his eyes; eyes disproportionately enlarged as it was. They were covered by a sort of opaque, secondary lid, which gave them the appearance of wet rounds of Weisslacker.

Further contributing to the matte of him, his countenance was dozed, so that the muscles sloughed faintly downward through the length of it, abbreviated drifts along a taper, creating the illusion that he was being floating by an invisible thread fastened to his forehead. At last, without the least bit acknowledging my presence, he arrived at the opening in the aft, standing just over me. He took the rigid manner of a century post, those enameled eyes peering into the moonlit meadow, unflinching.

Not wanting to startle him, I whispered, "Jacob, are you alright?"

The boy's full inventory of senses appeared reallocated to sight, so that I was quite certain he hadn't heard my voice at all. My repeated asking did not raise any response, so deep was he in that mix of sleep and guarding. Close enough to ensure he would come to no harm, I surrendered to the scene as an observer.

His gaze was fixed, unbroken, upon a dimly penumbra, which leached from the great darkness behind the distant tree bluff. The sepia toned puddles of shadow that collected around the ankles of those trees, looked as dropped forest trousers, which threatened to trip the grove. The combination of his haunted manner and that creeping gloom across the meadow, gave rise to goose flesh for the length of me, as I was certain Jacob knew the grim something to come.

"Jacob, you're sleepwalking. Can you hear me? Jacob."

He then turned to me, the unfocused carriage of his face looking absolutely through me, and he reached over my shoulder, even grazing my ear. I reached up to shake him gently, but his trance proved so competent, that I was no threat to it whatever. When he stood erect again, he had retrieved his arm from behind my shoulder, and was then holding a large hammer, which fell limply to his side, the weight of unresisted iron.

All instinct in me could sense some dawning terror, so I reached quietly for my spear, never taking my eyes from the boy. As I moved into a position behind him, careful not to disturb, I was immediately braced by the scent of the beast. Unlike the dim, dissolving sigh that I had caught upon my first arriving there, the musk was rising, until it steadied itself to one pitch. The cat was near, then still and silent in the mead, I was confident, just outside the plane.

Looking out the portal, beyond Jacob, forgiving night breezes were drifting across the waist high grasses, delivering from their shoulders, a merciful drop in temperature. I too, like Jacob, found myself peering into the meadow, though my senses had become a posse formed only for the bounty on that prowling nemesis of mine. Time was lost to me, searching the clearing, until the silence and our meditation was shattered--

"Father, Father, she's coming!" Jacob screamed frantically.

Upon the snapped silence, adrenaline radiated to the corners of me. The pilot did not stir in the cockpit, as dead men never do. I put my hand upon my brother's shoulder, assuring him, "Jacob, Jacob, I am here with you. Tell me what is happening?"

Jacob remained deaf to my voice and unresponsive to my touch. The pilot was still not moving or responding, and the smell of that cat was so prominent, through the yard, still invisible.

Jacob became increasingly agitated, nearly hysterical, thrashing about in caged panic. His eyes were still of that dull, pearly caliber, dragging the whole of his head in a wake behind them, his face skyward and craning, as a blind man! He screamed, "Father, she's there! I feel her! She's coming! Help me!"

My gaze re-cocked to the perimeter, where I detected something; something moving between the hedge of those trees.

A silhouette, two-legged and vertical, weaving between the trees, alternating hands rolling across the barrels of those trees, as it slalomed. As if lost, the figure lyrically called, as if a child playing a game of hide and seek, "Biiiggggg boooyyyyy..where are you? Biiiggggg boooyyyyy!" The call of that translucent form careened the amphitheater of the clearing, muted as it met the blunt of the forest perimeter.

The figure suddenly stopped, registering sight of the plane, as it appeared. As it stepped into the moonlight, it moved like a tall bird, an ostrich or some such, toes grounded and heels raised. The face of the thing was swiveling manically, like a jackal collecting windswept intelligence. It also was human in some qualities, a woman maybe, and then her head locked on Jacob in the doorway. The thing then furiously was clawing at the earth beneath it, throwing up a plume of heavy earth.

It...she...it emerged into the clearing with modest first steps, but without warning, it burst to a fierce ground speed, which melted in the blur of a rifle ball approaching at a right angle to our craft! Nothing human was moving at that speed, thought I! As the conclusion was still emerging from my mind, the creature squealed at a tortured pitch, "Jaaaaaccccoooooooobb!"

The blood had long drained from Jacob's face. "Jacob, who is that?! Jacob?!"

𝔅𝔦𝔫𝔤𝔢

"The door! Close the door!" Jacob screamed.

He furiously pulled a tenured sheet of wood across the opening in the fuselage, semi-securing us inside, as I did what I could to help brace it there! He screamed, "The nails, Esau! The nails!!!"

In a crude pile lay a collection of nails, bent and rusted from what I assumed to be repeated use. I handed them to Jacob and he like journeyman, made quick work of securing that makeshift panel.

I took a position at one of the portholes, looking out at the ghoulish image, which had arrived at the closed hatch. First glance indicated that she was some quasi-human form, female in her sex. She was sniffing at the ground and the openings in our semipermeable plank, as a hound with the smell of a rabbit, deeply nostrilled.

As she raised her head, so that her face could be seen, I reacted in appropriate horror, as she, like the mythological Janus, wore a double frontispiece! It was not the single face cleaved, but rather, her neck was the pedestal for two busts. One face, quite normal, was that of a pretty, middle aged woman, looking straight forward, as a million before her. However, at a horrifying orientation to the pleasant face, sitting atop her collar at ninety degrees, was the mask of some ghoul from hell, which worked to form that horrifying duplex. The foundation of the second face was precisely that of its neighbor, clearly having begun within the human category of identical twins. But some assault of terror had been so delivered upon it over a series of misfortunes, which had rendered it to such a state that I could neither bare to look at it, nor could I turn away. I simply found myself frozen there, allowing my conscience to be seared by the presentation.

The skin of that second face was thick and white, powdery white, as if blood had been wrung from it and then replaced with sap. The eyes were electric and icy blue, the iris ringed in a thick rope of black. These features, child's play, in context, for in great diamond shapes about those sockets, the flesh had been peeled back at such a depth, that the fibrous musculature beneath was exposed, revealing deep scarlet slicks, as if she had awakened in the midst of her own autopsy. The flesh of the upper lip had melted into long, rotted flaps, which viewed in sum, dangled like a moustache; a vibrissa formed from the carcass of a squid, discreting her lower lip. All appearance, aggravated by the tumult of its mood. It was...cranky for the boy.

It wailed, "Jacob..! Jacob...! I'm coming in!"

Jacob had dissolved into agony, shaking and curled into that kinder-knot, his back against that makeshift drawbridge, trying to keep that creature from breaking into the craft. He was breathless and seizing, looking up to me, desperate, but unable to speak.

I screamed through the paneling, my spear at the ready, should that thing burst through, "I tell you I will drop you where you stand, you fiendish cunt!"

The creature was powerful, so powerful, and I could not be sure that as I said it to him "Jacob, listen to me. Nothing is going to happen. I'm here now. I can protect you. I've got you. I've got you."

The Jacob I had been with was gone from his face, leaving only the wake blood rage welling in the vacancy of those eyes. He was in a full seizure and I could do nothing, fully deployed as I was to keep that freak from breaching the portal.

The woman was scratching, not to be ignored, at the makeshift panel across the plane's opening. Through a small opening, she rifled a gangly and filthy arm, which caught purchase of the boy's leg. As she grabbed with fury, she spun him on his seat, and then made haste to pull his tiny legs through the serration of that plywood barrier. As he clung to the base of those seats, he became both the rope and the contestant, in a human tug of war. His little legs were being torn apart, sending long, deep stripes into the length of them. So, I discovered, that is where those myriad lashings had formed.

I grabbed his hand and we locked eyes, but the strength of that cunt was nearly overpowering two of us, and worse still, unless one of us let him go, he would be severed within moments. I was crazed, desperate, about to surrender my grasp upon him, when that wonderful companion, that geyser of rage, plumed in me. A clarity had come, a remembrance of the cat, certainly nearby in the meadow. With some power, which I cannot say for certain was me, I focused my full being upon calling to that cat for rescue. With the full power of my mind's eye, I willed that cat, come!

When I reached the full pitch of my concentrated rage, my blood at a rolling boil, I heard a terrific ROOOOOOOAAAAAAAARRRRRRR outside the plane. The sound of that cat's battle cry was in our hearing, the woman's hand released the boy slowly....and slowly withdrew from the hole in the panel. I retrieved Jacob, pulling the boy across the floor to me, where he was a huddled, blood-soaked; a mass, streaked in tears of terror.

I rose to look out the port window, to find the wonderful Jaguar was in full flight behind the woman, who was moving at equally high speed into the distant clearing.

The boy there on the floor, desperately clawing for that orange crayon, which he had hurtled during the scrum. I collected it I handed it to him, which he pulled close to his chest, as a child comforted by its blanket. He then rocked and held his head in my lap, brushing his hair with my hand, to

BINGE

calm him. "Jacob, I am here, now. This will never, never, never happen again. I'm, I am here. I will never let this happen again. I will take you from here, my brother. Esau has you now. Esau has you now. Esau has you now."

The boy finally was calmed, though the damage to him was severe. I rested his head upon a pile of laundry, covering him in the best I could find to form a blanket. I rose, horrified and confused, with no idea whatever, as to what I had just witnessed.

As I stared out the porthole, I could see the cat was returning from across the meadow, toward our position. He moved with grace and calm, until he finally arrived just outside the plane. After pacing the length of the plane several times, a soldier protecting its fort, it came to sit steadfastly, daring all comers to approach the plane. I knew that that beast would kill me, sure as it would have killed that woman, but it was clear that it had some affection for the boy. And, that there was some unspoken connection between the cat and me, which I felt as sure as I was breathing.

As I surveyed the scene about me...the damaged boy on that floor...the pilot, dead in the cockpit...that cat, faithful at post... and myself, even, staring through that window and into the distant tree bluff, searching for that two-faced cunt...I uttered, "What in the hell was that...?"

And, a reply came through the still air of the plane, "His mother."

It was the pilot, resurrected...

CHAPTER 21

NO
RECORD OF WRONGS

acob had assured me that I would see for myself, and I did. Impossible as it was to believe, the man, who was breathless there for over twelve hours, was breathing and speaking, as if nothing had ever happened to him. I left Jacob in the back of the plane, taking a position in the copilot's seat, next to the resurrected pilot.

"Sir, the boy, sir...sir very bad shape." I said quietly, so as not to disturb Jacob's resting.

"Yes, Esau. You are right to say that he is."

"I've covered him up and he's resting at the back of the plane."

"Yes, yes, I know. Under the blankets.... Laundry as a pillow. I know." He said, as if the information was all rote for him.

"Yes, sir. That is exactly what I was about to say." I responded, equally surprised was I by the cavalier expression, as by his telepathy.

"And, the crayon, Esau? Did he demand the crayon?" he impatiently insisted, as if I should have known to offer the information on my own.

"He did, sir, yes."

The pilot withdrew into himself for a moment, wincing almost, notably disappointed in my answer to him.

Sighingly, "Indeed, Esau. He still cannot be without the crayon."

"Yes, I think that might be true."

"You don't think he's ready...to be without the crayon?"

"I...I don't know. I just know that he was desperate for it and that's what finally calmed him down."

"Did you offer him this crayon OR did he ask for it?" he tarried.

"He was clawing the floor to get to it. I retrieved it for him." I responded sharply. I was becoming frustrated with his focus on the seemingly meaningless detail, given that his son had nearly been killed moments earlier.

"I wished that he could let go of that crayon." he said, lost in the wish.

"The crayon, sir?! The crayon?! I don't think you understand what has happened to this boy! The crayon is not the problem."

"Esau, the crayon IS the problem. It's as simple and impossible as that crayon he keeps." He paused, as if he was saying something that was actually true…even profound. "And, what, Esau, of his Mother?"

"It was not his mother, sir, I can assure you. It was a beast of some kind. It was finally chased--"

"Yes. Yes. Chased away by the cat." he said, again finishing my sentence exactly as I had intended to do, BEFORE I had finished with it.

"Sir, how could you know all that has happened here? You are…you were… dead…blind."

"Jacob is always there this time of day. After his mother comes. Holding his crayon and sleeping, just so. It has always been thus. And, may always be."

"That cannot be true, sir. This beast who came, the one you call Mother, she is more powerful than I. She had the strength of ten men. Had I not been here to fight for him, she would have taken him...easily."

"Yes, yes. This. Yes. this is true. But, you were here... and you did fight. Tell me more of this fight, boy."

"She came… she tried to pull the boy from the plane. She got hold of him, but I was able to grab him too, to keep her from taking him away."

"And, when you were holding on to him...what happened?"

"I held him as long as I could do, but she was so powerful, I found I couldn't...I, I couldn't keep on. I knew that I would lose him."

Frustrated by my answer, "No, Esau!" he said severely. "What happened to Jacob, when you were holding on to him, as you were?"

"He was being torn in half. It was terrible. He was in such pain, sir. Suffering..." I said, deeply recalling the expression of Jacob helplessly looking for me to rescue him during the incident.

"Ah, yes. Maybe there is good in this, after all."

I reacted in revulsion at his comment, "Good? Good, you say? This is a terrible thing which has happened. If this is good, you must tell me what is there that is good in it?"

Nonplussed, he offered simply, "The suffering."

"The suffering is good? No, the suffering is not good. Sir, if you could have seen what transpired. If you could only see your son."

"You see this suffering, Esau. That makes the suffering... perfect."

I tried to collect myself, at the face of that pilot's insanity, but before I could respond, he added an even more disturbing commentary.

"And, Esau, you see your fault in all this suffering, yes?" he said.

"My fault? No! I see that without me he would have been killed. All due respect to you, sir, for you suffer, too, but this woman, this creature, this beast is...powerful...and terrifying...and--"

"Yes, yes, yes...'this creature is evil...this creature has two faces. Yes, I know what you are going to say, Esau, before you say it."

I was dazed. For, the third time, he had finished my sentence precisely as I intended to do. He had spoken words that had been formed in my mind, but had not yet made passage to my tongue.

"You know, that is exactly what I was about to say, don't you?"

"Yes."

"How do you know what I am going to say before it is said, then?"

"You don't know I know?"

"Of course not."

"And, your mind...? What of your mind, Esau?"

"My mind, sir, is damaged, I would say, and beyond repairing. Erased, in fact. I have no memories at all. I have only some dim

BINGE

awareness that Jacob is my brother, but it is only an instinct, nothing more. As for all other things I might ever have known before, which include my own identity, I know nothing."

His opaqued eyes filled with tears and his comprehensive expression announced a great relief and gratitude. I marked that as the greatest confusion, at that time, in the bush.

"What you now say, Esau, you see, has made me very happy. Very happy, indeed."

"Sir, what of my added suffering, to the suffering of this place, could possibly make you happy?" I said, exasperated.

"That your suffering, Esau, it only exists in this moment and no place else."

"And, you are happy with of this, of course."

"I am happy, for you, Esau. For, it is forgetting that will be required to heal my son. Time and forgetting. Time and forgetting. Time and forgetting."

"Nothing of what you say makes any sense to me. I want to help you, do you understand? I want to help, but these things you saying are not helping me help the two of you."

"You mean, 'the three of us'."

"You and your son are two."

"And Mother makes three."

"Mother?! That creature in the field, is the one you call Mother. You can't mean her."

"But, I do."

"I will kill her, should she come near this boy again. I shall fill her with this pike of mine, I promise."

"No, Esau. Her, too. You can't save me...you can't save my son...unless you save Mother, too."

"But, Jacob is all that matters, yes?"

"Yes, it is as you say."

"Then I must take him far from this place. Right away, I must take him."

"Yes. But, he won't go. My son must choose to go. You see?"

𝕭𝖎𝖓𝖌𝖊

"Then he must be told, sir. You must tell him he must leave this place."

"Yes, I have told him, but he won't go. He won't leave me. And..." he said, leading me.

It was upon on me, the realization, as if I was catching a ball of thought, which the pilot had tossed to me, "And...so, you cannot...pass."

"That's right. I cannot die, Esau. And so, I will suffer. And this boy, he will suffer. And Mother..."

"She suffers...?"

"She does. That creature you see in her, that is not her. She wears two faces, but it was not always so. This second face you have seen, this is the face for me, not for the boy."

"What do you mean, 'the face for you?'"

"This boy, he only sees one more face. He sees the face of his mother, as she has always been to him. The mother loves him, cares for him and wants him with her. But, this second face, is the face Jacob never sees. This is the face that grows just for me. Like her face before, only rotted by time and hatred, until it has become a face all its own."

I was lost, but also confident that it was not for me to respond in any way, but to simply listen and let the madness wash over me.

"It's been thirty years, Esau. I know that I have no power to fix this."

"You are lamed, sir. But, I am here now, to help in this."

"Are you, Esau? Have you come here, at last, to end this suffering?"

"Tell me, sir. Tell me what I can do, so that this boy will understand what must be done?"

The man reacted with a deep, cleansing breath, as if I had said precisely what he needed to hear. As if I had uttered a password of some kind.

"I think, you really mean this, Esau. I think you are ready. I pray, you are ready now."

"Tell me what it is, please sir. I beg you. I will do what you say I must, if only the boy can be free of this place."

The pilot collected himself and then his voice moved from inquisitive to intense, to a kind of...tenderness, as if speaking to me, he was speaking to a child.

"Esau, my dear, Esau. You are a good boy. A very good boy. You must listen to me now and you must do as I tell you. You are right to say the boy must leave this place. And, the boy alone, must decide to leave the place."

"Yes, Jacob must be told then. We must make Jacob understand that he cannot stay here another day."

The pilot was silent for a long time. Then, delicately, as if he was sneaking up to whisper into the ear of a fawn, he spake thus, "Esau, Esau, it is not Jacob who holds us here."

"You just said it is the child who must choose." I said, though I did it as if I was trying to reclaim ground, which was eroding from beneath my feet.

"You see that we each suffer, but do you see the way in which we suffer?"

"I see only suffering. Help me see."

"We are each, mitred, Esau. Each split in his own way. I am snapped in half at the leg, but also I am half dead and half living. Yes? The boy, my son, his mother is split, too. You have seen that she wears these two separate faces, so at war is she, within herself. Even this very plane, Esau. Even this place, you can see, put us under."

"Yes, I see."

"We each are cleaved in our own way. And, only the child can spare us."

"Only Jacob? Only Jacob is NOT split."

"No, Esau. Jacob, too. He has suffered the worst of the curse in this place. For, Jacob, has suffered the greatest split of any."

"How does Jacob, my brother, suffer this curse?"

"The man who authors this curse, he is the man for whom we all suffer."

"Where is this man, who causes my brother to suffer so?! I shall find him by dawn and bring you his head on this pike!"

"Esau, Esau, you will find this man, wherever you will find this boy."

He was agitated, reaching for a small log book, which was resting on the plane's console. I grabbed the book and handed it to him.

"Thank you, but that book is not for me. That book belongs to you."

BINGE

"To me, sir?"

"In that book, you will find this man you seek."

I took the book from him, unwrapping the tie at the binding, releasing the cover and opening it slowly. As I was staring down into the pages of the book, my bowels turned to water.

"You see now, my Esau? You see this man you seek?"

I could not speak, for there inside the book was no writing, but only A MIRROR, which provided a horrifying reflection back to me. It was a face far more horrifying than the face of that beast they called Mother, for this face was but a full face which had been deeply cleaved down the center, so that it was splayed in half completely. This face was my own face! I reacted in horror at the sight of this monstrosity staring back at me! I slammed the book shut and was breathing heavily.

"You see, Esau? You have seen this man."

"What have I seen, Sir? What is this horror that I have seen?!

"This man, Esau, this man who alone can end this suffering..."

"Yes...?"

"Esau, you are this man."

"Me? How? What? This can't be. It is Jacob, you said. It is Jacob who must leave this place of his own choosing!"

"There is no Jacob, Esau. You are Jacob."

"No! No! This is impossible! This can't be!" The world was spinning wildly, so that my balance was lost to me.

The pilot pressed in on me with his speaking, "You say, Esau, that Jacob is at the back of this plane, but I say to you, Esau, Jacob is standing here before me."

I looked...I looked madly down the plane, where the boy was in the fetal position, nursing those wounds, catatonic, and he was gone! When I looked down to my legs, they were covered in the lashes and stripes of that conflict.

Burrowing in on me, he said, "You say, Esau, that Jacob clutches the crayon in his hand, but I say to you, it is you who are standing before me, clutching this crayon as you speak."

Terrified to look, I finally looked down to find that, in fact, the crayon was buried tightly in my clenched fist!

"Esau, you say that these marks on the walls and the skin of this plane are marks counting the days, but I say to you, look closer Esau. You must look closer, my child. Because...you are almost there..."

My senses were flooded, overcome, and my head was spinning and my hearing dimmed. As I entered the cabin to observe all of those tick marks, they were not tick marks at all, but letters. Words. A word. Written over and over and over and over again.

"Can you see it, Esau? Can you see what you have written there..?"

I uttered, choking on it, as I did, "Vergeben."

"Yes, Esau, yes! This is the word! This is what needs to be done to end this suffering. This word alone, spoken only by you, will end this pain forever...for all of us."

"Vergeben...FORGIVE...FORGIVE...FORGIVE."

I knew it was true, that I was this man. I knew this word, which I had written over and over again. I knew that this crayon belonged to me. And, I knew that I had been trapped inside this place for those thirty years and a day. I collapsed to my father's knees, sobbing, as the dam in me had been broken.

"Esau, Esau, my son. We have all been split, but you have been split worst of all. For, you Esau, have been split in the mind. You are this savage, who is thirty years gone from here. But, you are also this small boy, who never left."

I was dissolved at his feet, sobbing.

"You have been a good boy. You are a good man. My son, this stepped forward is one single step...for which you have been prepared this lifetime. Take, this step."

He was petting my head; I was overcome in the shock of all that I had suddenly realized.

"This answer to this suffering, my son, is not force. You cannot kill this with your spear. You cannot take this through the strength of your arms. What you are hunting for is Peace. And peace comes through one act alone. Vergeben. Forgiveness."

"No! No! I won't do it! I won't!"

"You must, Esau. When you forgive...I can rest. You must do this for me...for us, my son."

My eyes deliquesced again, awash in tears and the flood of memory returning to me. My father...my mother...the crash.

"We've all suffered quite enough and now you must be find it in yourself to let this pain go."

"Oh, Father, no. No."

"You can do this, Esau. You are Big Boy and you can do this for me. For all of us who suffer."

"I can't let you go.

"Forgive your mother, Esau. Forgive yourself. And let me rest, my child. Let us all rest this day."

He pulled my head into his lap and was stroking it, as I cried and cried, a river of tears. And he just kept repeating the same thing over and again..."

"Let it all go, boy...let it all go...forgiveness is letting it all go....

"I do! I do! I do! I forgive...I forgive...I forgive...I forgive..."

And with the words and that torrent, so too did his hand finally come to a complete rest, there upon my head. I could feel his spirit had left the place...and, me along with it.

I rose from my position there on the floor, standing then, over the broken body of my father. He was gone, but gone too was his suffering. I removed his glasses from his face and returned them to him, leaving him in the tableau, which I had loved most: that of the pilot. I kissed him, tenderly as I could do, upon his head, one last time.

I emerged from the cockpit, entranced and numb, entering the empty cabin of the plane. It was strange to feel it so deeply, but looking into that empty pile of blankets, there where I had last seen Jacob, reminded me that I had not only lost my father, but that little boy, too. Even if he had only been some imagining of mine, I missed him just the same. To this day, even now, I am still comforted by knowing that in my darkest hour of need, the one truth that sustained me, was there in the face of my brother sleeping. While Jacob may not have lived past that night in the plane, dissolving into the ether with my memory of my father, that damask of virtue as he slept, has remained real and important and with me, as any realer thing has ever done.

It was true, as it came to pass, that in watching him sleep, I was seeing the best of myself.

After those few moments in the cavern of that fuselage, contemplating all that had transpired there, I resolved myself to one unfinished act. I took the few steps forth to the bulkhead, behind the cockpit, where those thirty years' orange tick marks were scrawled. And there, upon my tipped toes, with that little orange crayon, I left my final marks upon the craft. In the hand of that child, always in the hand of that child, I wrote the words: IT IS FINISHED.

CHAPTER 22

HOLY GROUNDS

ometimes, the place becomes more than a place, sacred, imbued with a spirit beyond itself. Burial sites, are such as these. So, too, are places of great sacrifice or tragedy, altered forever in this way. Holy grounds. Such was that wreckage for me, a holy place. It was hard for me to leave it, though there was nothing left for me inside; save those faces, still undissolved, and the memories of their voices, still in my hearing. My father's wisdom, passed to me. The damask, that veil of virtue over Jacob's sleeping face. And, my own best self had been therein, called to the breach, to protect them both to my own death, and happily. Leaving all of that behind was impossible and necessary. For in the end, the place where they had lived, was not in that clearing, but in some vast and unhealed trench within me.

Such were my final thoughts, as I stood there in the rent of the side of that plane. Beneath the soft light of that waxing moon, I could see three figures waiting patiently afield. None amongst them making any move toward me, nor were their gestures suggestive to any kind violence, which that creature had announced before it previously charged. They were simply a tiny tribe, collected loosely there, waiting, as silhouettes of peace. The ambience of the meadow whole, had been recast, then void of the hostility, which had hitherto punished it so. Peace awaited its completion, that single act from me, the capstone which would sustain the arc above us all. Forgiveness.

My psychological and emotional reality was, and is, not simple. It was not, for me, the ease of throwing a switch inside myself, which would allow me to complete this wish of my father. Profound doubt was in me, outwardly manifest as lead in my soles, making those first few strides forth, clumsy and heavy. The blessing from my father, however, was extended to me as a form of spiritual lending, where the balance due, was in that remaining act of mine: to forgive.

I emerged from the plane, at last, dim footed, landing upon the porch where the cat had previously stood guard over Jacob. As my feet made contact with that hallowed ground, they fell into the enormous cast of that jaguar's prints. I was grateful for his ethic in that conflict, protecting Jacob, when I could not do. The confusion in me was only amplified, as in protecting Jacob, he was, in fact, protecting some part of me. It was at the moment, when the relationship with the jaguar came to exist someplace between the tip of my spear and the depth of my gratitude.

His pungence was ripe and constant to me then, which indicated both his stillness and proximity. A quick survey of the meadow perimeter produced a view of him, sitting patiently, at a safe distance, completing a triangle between he, my mother and me.

In addition to the crayon, I had kept the small book that my father gave me, in hand. The book, containing only that single page, which was that mirror. Tremulous, I opened the book again, fortified as I could be, for the horror which might present in my waiting reflection. As I looked down into the mirror again, I was overwhelmed with relief, to find that my face had been restored to a normal structure, no longer cleaved down the center. The face looking back at me, however, was caked in blood and sweat and the patina of that jungle silt. Again, it was marvelous. After a long drink of that reflected savage, I closed the book and tossed it into the wreckage. My time there was done.

Turning my back upon the plane, I began to make my way across the clearing, to where those silhouettes stood waiting. My eyes toggled, as much deployed on that cat, as they were upon the family there. My spear, as ever, was ready at my side, prepared for even a twitch from him. The journey through that meadow to that doorway of my destiny, carried with it the tension of a ransom delivered in exchange for a life.

As I arrived near to them, without incident, it was, indeed the woman, my mother, though she was no longer that terrifying creature. As my father had said, I was seeing the face, which I was intended to see: 'the mother's face', the view reserved for the child alone. This woman, whom I did not recognize in that previous altercation, was then well known to me, for she was most certainly my mother. Though all recollections of mine were sparse and rusted, there was no mistaking her, for that the face I had just seen reflected back at me in that mirror was a face I positively inherited from her.

Mother was flanked by two other characters, one of whom was a man of great height and the other of whom was a little girl, sweetly faced and pigtailed. These faces, again, were familiar to me, but through the gauze of my damaged recall.

"Christopher?" Mother asked of me, delicately, her voice a combination of her near fulfilled hopes and the struggle for recognition. "I don't believe it, my Christopher."

For all that had happened in the plane, where I had been called Esau and also Jacob, I left the wreckage behind, and I left as a unified person once more, whom I knew to be this man she called Christopher.

BINGE

Her eyes were filled with uncried tears, as she then took cautious steps to meet me. She stood her distance, though a powerful maternal gravity was acting upon her with each step I took forth. I could see that she was desperate to draw me into to her embrace, but I was cautious, some deep scarring of mine, which made the prospect of intimacy with her, very difficult. Were it not for the urging of that promise I made to my dying father AND the message that had been scrawled on that plane for thirty years, I may have stood that single step from her, forever.

"Oh, Christopher," she cried, "I thought I had lost you forever." I looked into her longing eyes, longing for me to close the distance of that single step to meet her in embrace. I was equally focused to the view over her shoulder, where the tall man and the little girl were standing respectfully.

The man's face, I remembered dimly, as the copilot during the crash. My father's best friend. While unspecific, my sense of him was one of affection, though any specific memory had been lost with the rest of that inventory. And the little girl...the little girl was my sister. The one affectionately called 'Grangey'. The poor thing was broadcasting such fear and timidity through those sweet eyes of hers, as well she should have done at the sight of me, armed and primitive as I was.

Looking gently to her, as I could manage, I choked out, "Grangey, Father... Our...father...he is gone now."

She looked up to me, her gentle eyes indicating her understanding, such as it could be at a tender age.

Mother was nodding her head in proxy, still in the manner of not knowing what to say to me, in a moment where there is nothing one can say.

"We know, sweetheart. We know that Joe is gone. I'm so sorry."

I was dissolving inside, at the sound of her voice, on the verge of breaking down there in front of them. The feeling inside me was much the feeling I had during that terrible conflict, when I couldn't hold on to Jacob any longer.

One step forth to her was all that separated me from fulfilling my father's wish, but it was no ordinary step. If was for not the promise made to him, I believe I should have stayed there in my anger and pride and resentment for a lifetime. As it was, I took the single step, which is always the distance to forgiveness, and my torn and broken body fell into her waiting arms. In those arms, amidst that sea of tears, a thousand miseries and angers were washed from me.

"My Christopher, my darling boy. I've got you now."

After a long while, she withdrew from me, quickly noticing the Saint Christopher medallion about my neck. As she brushed it sentimentally between her thumb and forefinger, her recognition of the charm delivered the bitter-sweetness of love lost to time.

"It was Muzzy's." I said. "I've kept it, for luck, I think. Or, maybe..."

"...Or maybe, so that you would never forget how much she loved you, when you were so awfully much alone."

"Yes. To never forget that love from her. My greatest love was for her. I am sorry and also not so sorry, as I say this to you, Mother."

"Shhh...shhh, Christopher. It's alright. This step is behind you now. This single step, which has been a lifetime to take. There, there, now. You know that your father would say to you now? Time and forgetting, Christopher. Time and forgetting. Time and forgetting."

The man standing behind, stepped forward, and as he came into the advantage of the moonlight, he was holding a large dagger in his hand. I withdrew at once from my mother, raising my spear to him, instinctively.

"No, Christopher. This is only, Rolf. You remember Rolf, don't you?" she asked.

My eyes were fixed more upon the dagger than the man. He spoke to me in his heavy German accent, "Ah, Christoph, you always loved this knife."

He offered the dagger in his upturned palm, where it rested unthreateningly. As the moonlight caught the fuller, it distributed the amplified moonlight in all directions around us.

"Christoph..." he said, "Take this dagger from me. You are not a boy anymore. This belongs to you now."

I stared at his gentle face, that kind face behind the dagger, while the sound of his voice was over me like the dust of a fairy. In that moment of stillness, I knew it. That was the dagger, which had marked the way for me...back to my father in that plane. Invisible was this man's hand, but ever present was he, in the fulfilling of my destiny and healing.

"It was you...who marked my way. It was you, invisibly guiding me."

"Chrisoph, it was not only me, it was me and him. Your father and me, too. Your father was a good man...and a good friend. But, life is not perfect. So, people get hurt. Children get hurt. And, fathers, too."

"What is this etching, carved into the blade? I cannot see this marking under the moonlight."

"It is the word ZWEITER. I put it there, for you."

"The second?"

"Yah. This is what I am, boy. Second. Turn it over. On the other side, it says Erste."

Translating, I uttered, "First."

"Christoph, you are very lucky boy. Very lucky. What boy can say, he has two fathers who love him? You, you are such a boy as this."

He was right and I knew that I was no longer torn in conflict, but restored as he told me. "Yes, two fathers. I know you are right. I am this lucky boy, who can say this thing."

As I was mesmerized by that shining blade, the jaguar was restless in the distance, up and prowling, as if to tell me he had waited long enough.

Looking to my mother, I said, not unkindly, "My father was a good man. He deserved better, I think."

"He did. I know. I am so sorry, Christopher. I don't think I knew until now..." she was staring at the wreckage in the field, "I don't think I knew until now, how much Joe really loved me."

"How is that?" I asked.

"All those years alone. He never...he never recovered from that crash. He never moved on, as we did. In the end, he suffered in the loss of his own life, and in that loss, we have all been restored to one another."

"Yes, Mother. This, which you say to me now, this is all I need. Maybe, all I ever needed. There will be no more suffering... for any of us. No more suffering for me. In this forgiveness, which I have promised to my father and myself, I say to you, it is finished."

I looked to the little girl, shyly standing at the distance and signaled her, "Come here to me, Grangey."

She was reluctant, until Mother encouraged her, "It'll be alright, Grangey. This is your brother, Christopher. He won't hurt you."

She stepped forward and I towered over her. As she looked up to me, her expression was very much like the face of Jacob. That wonderful mix of longing and innocence, which together are some mysterious recipe for kindness. I reached up behind my neck, releasing the Saint Christopher chain. Lowering myself to one knee, at eye level with her, I worked to fasten it upon her tiny frame. My filthy, war torn hands, contrasted there against her tenderness, I pray I shall never forget that sight, for it is the image of the purpose beneath the savagery in me. "I believe that you are the one who should wear this charm, which belonged to our Grandmother. Yes? Muzzy loved us Grangey. Let this charm remind you of her protecting us as we travel our different paths. Let it remind you that we started together and that I am never so far away that I can't hear you calling. You understand this, yes?"

She nodded, still voiceless. "There's a good, lass, now. You will be safe with Rolf and Mother. You will all be safe now. She scampered back to Rolf's side.'

"Where will you go, Christopher?" my mother asked.

I was staring off in the distance at the cat, who had extended all the courtesy I had needed then. "There is something waiting for me, Mother. Something I must finish, now and alone."

I fastened the dagger at my waist, to my loin cloth.

I pulled my mother close to me, "You understand now, Mother. It is finished. It is all finished. This curse is upon us no more. I wish for you to live in peace."

"I love you, Christopher. I will always love you, my Big Boy."

"And, I you, Mother. Good-bye...for now."

My mother returned to my second father and my sister, and the three of them dissolved hand in hand, into the inky darkness behind the treeline there. The voice of the jaguar came softly over the mead, a gentle reminder that his patience was spent.

At last, I was standing alone, eyes upon the wreckage and meditating upon one last good-bye, yet spoken. Still clutched there, in my right hand, was my little crayon. Father had told me, which confused and frustrated me greatly when he said it, "Esau, Esau, that crayon IS the problem. It is as simple and as impossible, as that crayon he keeps." I understood then, standing there in the wake of that reconciliation. The crayon was the instrument of my imprisonment, in this sense: it was through that child's implement, that I worked to record, over and over again, that thirty-year record of wrongs. Every stroke from that crayon, was my effort to cling to that pain. Every scrawl from me became yet another bar in the cage of bitterness in which I lived so long. And, it was a self-made prison, which kept me from the experience peace and love. That little crayon made had impossible for me to heal, for as my father said best, healing only comes with, "Time and forgetting. Time and forgetting. Time and forgetting."

I dropped the wax marker to the earth, just beneath me, and with my leathery foot, I buried it in the soil. As that crayon was put us under, I stared out at the wreckage mid field, one last tear bled from my eye and fell the distance from my cheek to the floor of that clearing.

As that silver tear met the earth, there was a great crack of thunder and a shard of white lighting, which fell from the darkness of the heavens, grounding itself directly in the remains of my father's plane. The craft lit up in the smote, as a Roman Candle, the waste of it erased in a forgiving fire, until, at last, it became wonderful and twisting column of purple smoke, rising to the heavens.

As the fire dwindled, and the skies opened to pour forth a bowl of great rain upon that spot, dissolving forever, the site of that crash. Gone, was all of it, in mere moments, returned to the earth beneath it, where it would become fertile ground once more. Pain and death and forgiveness and fire...spiritual minerals each, which make possible a new life to come.

The clouds parted, sending a column of moonlight to the earth, as a spot light upon the cat, who was long past his waiting. Our eyes met, taught across the distance was our mutual gaze, and with the smallest signal from my eyes, I consented to him. Upon that instant, he sprung into flight, as did I, with a mind healed and free...thinking as I ran into the waiting jungle, what a beautiful night to die.

CHAPTER 23

THE ARROW THAT IS NOT AIMED

t was over bog and fallen tree and upon every offered vine, we flew, as long and lean, gorgeous muscle and mink. A slick energy had built between us, created by the invisible yoke about our pursuit. As we each asserted ourselves across and against the landscape, we became amplified, as it were. Our lithe bodies were only more so. Our keen knowledge of the jungle complex and our presence in it, only more so. It was if the vitality between us had underwritten a grace of movement beyond ourselves. We were two sinewed streaks of black and tan, which produced delicious breezes, bending softly, the forest there, to our drift. At last, the sweat that glazed our throttling bodies, glistened in variegated colors, so that the sheen upon us, came to appear as do slicks of oil upon thinly sleeping puddles. Ancient gods in flight, were we, in that wonderful labyrinthine steeplechase.

As sufficient as the push of force from the beast at my flank, there came also, a mysterious and equally magnificent, pull. By slow degrees, an audiomist rolled in across the jungle canopy, it came as a dimly music. With each powerful stride forth we took, the sound above us grew louder, its direction opposite to ours. It was the music of a native people, to be sure, the structure characterized by a nucleus of mania, drumbeats and thrashing feet, augmented by what I imagined to be the percussion of dried leaves, half shells and bones. The carnal power of those rhythms proved as beacon to both savage and beast alike, for with the steady beating of those drums, our hearts and strides melted into a synchronized cadence and bearing.

But, there was something ornamenting those baser aboriginal sounds, which was magnificently and deeply etched upon my recall. The collective sound that I have described thus far, earthy and ritualistic, it proved more a mere foundation for a much greater song to come. In gentle counterpoint to those prehistoric pulses, emerged a delicate and drifting voice, that of a woman, which floated above it all as a kind of melodic smoke. That singular voice drifted softly around and between those anchors of rhythm, as a morning mist surges into low pastures, arriving as billowing collars about hill and dale. The quality and deftness of that voice became a phonic center-point, which held the disparate sounds together in unified song.

It was then I believe, that I was completely lost. Not lost to the forest or to that clipping foe, but comprehensively lost to the moment. Surrendered. The best I can think to describe it, is to say that I had forfeited my interest in outcome, trading it instead for the freedom of experiencing being fully alive. The samurai speak of 'the arrow that is not aimed', as the quiet and complete surrender to the mysterious force that shapes the destiny of all living things. The archer, his eyes closed, pulls the bow taught, the arrow is released without concern for its target, and without fail, each arrow arrives to its place of its final rest. So, too, was I such a pike, traveling in an unknown trajectory, to a certain destiny, at the will of forces beyond myself. And somewhere in flight, the husk of fear which had been so calcified to me, was shed, leaving in its stead, a perfect emptiness...a lightness of being...a quicksilvered peace. Were a weight assignable to fear, I cannot imagine it as more that of a sigh, but when the weight of fear has gone, it must be equivalent to the loss of one's entire self.

Into that empty space, which fear no longer occupied, surged a spring of joy and love. Joy at the sound of my beating heart and the speed of foot and the dancing of that spear in my hand. And, of love, genuine love, it was focused singularly upon the cat on my heels. For, it was the cat who had mysteriously delivered me; the stealth engine behind my salvation. He was, at once, creature and collaborator. Predator and promise. Enemy and epiphany. As I flit across the brush, I came to wonder what it was I was really running from.

Without the least thought to it, I slowed my pace, allowing the jaguar to close much of the distance behind me, which he hungrily did. As his elongated frame was a mere body length from mine, I glanced over my shoulder, as he prepared to strike, and in that precise moment, I fell to one knee, as the cat moved over me in flight, sailing past me and tumbling headlong into the earth ten meters forth. I laughed and coaxed him to attack, "Come on, boy! Come and get me!"

The cat charged again and rather than running from him, which was my intuition to do, I drifted three lithe steps into his charge. In the milliseconds before promised collision, my eyes dissolved away the substance of him, for something much, much more valuable there. The great emptiness all around him, for he, as every substantial thing, was surrounded in all directions, by even more substantial pocket of negative space. Upon the moment of our colliding, I merely dove into one of those myriad pockets of emptiness, through which I moved as a whisper. He had missed again! With the deep laughter of that discovery, I was alight again, called ever forward by that music upon the air around us. The jaguar having tumbled behind me in a heap, recovered his footing, shaking his head and stretch as if his coat were filled with shame. And, off we flew again.

There was a new sound reaching prominence all around us, which was some yet visible water, gaining speed and rushing to a climax. The sound was the signature to far greater than a mere jungle vein or streamlet. This was the cacophonous and throaty roar of a great river opening onto a precipitous fall.

As the cat and I dashed the final cluster of high grasses and trees, we were come upon suddenly, by the literal end of the road. As we stopped short, our upper bodies heaving forth over our feet, we were peering over a magnificent and towering cliff, which was the pouting lower lip of an Amazonian waterfall. Great rock formations were as jagged teeth in the mouth of those falls, serving to make more of the turgid, great river, the moments before it met its punctuated end.

The cat roared in response to the angry voice of that river, reminding me, too, that no rest for the weary would be had. A collection of boulders was organized as a makeshift, though harrowing, natural footbridge across that river. Choice less, I stepped forth onto that rocky path, finding myself then in the very midst of the terrific aquatic rage. From my tenuous position there, looking down over the edge of those falls I could see column of white smoke drifting to the heavens and that music more prominent than ever in my hearing. As a man lost at sea for days, who finally catches sight of dry land, only to be drowned, so too was I so close and yet so far from the rescue of civilization. I was, at least, isolated mid-river, with that magnificent view of a safety I could not reach...a barefooted savage, upon a slick island of stone.

The cat was more cautious than I, taking reluctant initial steps into the aquafury, negotiating his way to that island of granite, upon which I stood.

"Come on, boy! You can do it! Come and I will finish you here on this perch, once and for all!" I shouted in pure joy and exhilaration, unable to wait for his arrival as the purity of the moment that I would slay him had come at last.

With those giant feet of his, he finally came to rest upon the floating stage with me, which platform was no more than five meters square. What a fitting arena for the tight and final combat between us, the result of which would end in the death of one, the other or both of us.

We began the dance from opposing ends of that stone, but by slow and methodical step, we each migrated to the center. As I arrived there first, I raised my cane spear to the approaching cat, to which he responded with a brief pause. In that pause, it occurred to me that to be armed in battle with that beast was not, well, it was beneath the dignity of the moment we had each longed for. In an act of pure savagery, I instead cast my spear over those great falls and watched it consumed by the furious mist thereover. Save the dagger at my hips, I was barehanded... and happily so.

The cat made its move on me, but again, my consciousness was keenly upon all of that empty space about him. As he

BINGE

approached, I resolved myself to stand within an abbreviated collar of a spot no larger than the plume of an umbrella. My territory was reduced to defending that tiny circle, in which I began to dance with him. My arms moved as blades on a windmill, my core bobbed like a cork bobbing in a stream, as I drifted through the beast over and again, using his force to cast him easily and repeatedly aside. The cat grew increasingly angry and frustrated, unable was he to so much as lay a paw upon me. He increased his fury and speed, until at last, he was no longer one cat, but appeared as three at once, moving in a wonderful blur around the stillness of me. The contrast in economies of motion was extreme, for he was such labor there and, I simply stood, a reed atop that furious waterfall, bending in the breeze of his passing.

The cat had exhausted himself and retreated to the edge of the great stone. "Is that all that you've got, boy?" I said joyfully. He was panting wildly and I stood waiting for him to reengage. He then laid down upon the great stone, spent and panting.

In the stillness of that moment, the two of us, upon that floating granite, in the heavens of that teeming waterfall, had reached the end. I reached for the dagger at my side, unsheathing it, wielding it in preparation for the kill. The beast rose to his feet in response. Rested and prepared for that final moment. It approached me and I stood my ground there at the edge of that stone, where I was but a stride from over the falls. That music from below was swelling and I had every confidence that the kill was mine to be had. One more clumsy leap from that cat and I would sink my dagger into his neck, as he passed through me. But, a most curious thing had happened to me. I had simply lost my taste for the kill of him. I had no need of it. The beast was magnificent and the taking of his life was the waste of something beautiful that had been with me in time...the equal of pulling the petals from a sleeping flower. There seemed something...nay, there was something, profoundly wrong with that final act.

I turned to the cat, a last moment, "You have been some kind of odd friend to me, Cat. There is some bond that unites you and me, which I now see. I cannot kill you, friend. I cannot do it to you...and you cannot help but do it to me. Should I stand here and surrender, you will take my life, for it is your nature. I cannot bide that either."

I sheathed my dagger to my side, which froze the cat in confusion. And, with two great strides to the edge of that stone, I leeeaaappptt over those falls! I screamed out and my cries echoed the forest around me. As I fell those first ten meters or so, I could see the cat's great black head peering over the precipice. I had left him to his life and I was myself, falling happily into the forever below, having chosen the manner of my death.

The cat then leapt, too! His fall, was at a rate much faster than mine. As he approached me, the two of us falling to what was to be our watery grave, I reached for him, grabbing the nape of his neck, and drifted over the top of him, straddling his great silhouette...falling...falling...falling through that fierce tears of that aquafjord.

As the bottom of the falls appeared, the churning and roaring turbulence met our eyes and ears. I dismounted the cat and we finally came to the pool below with a thundering crash.

As we submerged, we were each sent to the very bottom of the place, where rich layers of silt were stored, as underwater mattresses. In the carbonated chaos, he has disappeared from my view, as I discovered myself surrendered to a strange and powerful current at my feet. That force pulled upon me as a rope, delivering me into a deepset cave, until there was nothing, but to yield to the grave of it. And, I had been buried once again, without oxygen or rescue in sight. I was alive, underground.

CHAPTER 24

NINTH LIFE

s the whirlpool siphoned me through the airless crag of that underwater chamber, I traveled as a shell casing through a rifle's barrel, spiraling at high speed and involuntarily. I was being pulled backward and upward, at an increasingly severe diagonal, until, at last, I exploded through the taught pane at the water's surface, as a child borne breach. As I rose to the airy heavens, I did so in with the form of an inverted and corkscrewing Christ, my arms extended to the ferocious centripetal force, outward about the pin of my body. As a testament to the great force of that hydra which had sent me, I skyrocketed into the diaphanous curtains of the sky, well over twenty meters above the surface.

At the apex of my flight, I spent a fleeting moment in the invisible crow's nest between my rising and falling, far above the deck of that lake below. The body of the lake itself, from that aspect, appeared as if a journaling giant had spilled an inkwell, sending an abstract of blue black pigment across the skin of the earth, where it had collected forever in the low places, forming a magnificent body. Upon the great sheet of that black glass, which was the face of that lake, there was a softly concentric disturbance, the result of my breach, which rocked gently a tiny craft afloat thereon.

As I reentered the water, I was happily surprised by the substance of it, which more greeted me as a pool of mercury than water. The density and viscosity of that pool was a construct of some nobler form of liquid, to be sure. I was so at ease in the float of it, I was at last an unambitious buoy upon seawater, effortlessly bobbing, my full torso above the waterline, my waist forming a fleshy horizon between sea and sky. I happily reclined to the generosity, until I was irresistibly and effortlessly back floating, my ears enveloped beneath the soundless surface. Completely weightless and engulfed in the perfect quiet, I was a man at complete ease, afloat in God's very navel; a cosmic cork admiring that canopy of the night sky.

As I drifted thoughtlessly about the surface, I finally collided, gently collided, with a tiny vessel, which I had so drunkenly forgot was afloat with me on the aquaface. With no other soul in evidence there, it was more than strange to find that craft, which appeared waiting for my arrival there. As I inspected the hull of the orphaned punt, I discovered that it was fashioned in the manner and size of a modest canoe, though it was anything but a primitive craft. From that simple foundational form rose its elegant lines, the most prominent of which were discovered at its bow and stern, were asymmetrical serifs appeared upon that dreamy floating font. When viewed in its magnificent entirety, it was clear that only a swan sat for the sculpture, which was that punt. For there is nothing in creation to compare to the rising head of that majestic creature, which ascends deftly upon the elongated ess of its neck, turns upon itself to become a feathered treble clef and then disappears into the marvelous darkness of its nape. The beam of that tiny craft was much more the neck of that swan, for the artist's intention was only more clear for the presence of an unlit lantern, which hung about it as a necklaced jewel.

The density of that quicksilvered lake made easy ascent to the floating craft. I soft-footedly moved to the stem, where that lantern hung waitingly. As I began inspecting it, attempting to open the front panel, I was taken aback by the sudden glow it cast in response. Beginning as a faint glow and rising to a legitimate torchlight, I beheld in wonder that the lumens were being generated by a swarm of fireflies contained therein. My clumsy contact with the lamp had awakened a dreaming hive, who had taken to ambitious flight inside. As that light formed a sullen nimbus about my float, I gained a more informed view of that lake's dark face. With the advantage of that newly acquired aspect, just above the skin of the lamplit lake, I discovered a diversity of liquefied colors, pulsing upon the midnight lake, which was being generated by the wagging chin of my boat. As my eyes scouted the source of those myriad colors, they met with the view of vigorous banks in all directions, which were teeming with swaths of flowers and grasses. Those endless fields of wildflowers ashore, cast their pallet across the sleeping pond, until the mix of the two became a Monet, painted upon a canvass of black vinyl, upon and amidst which I floated.

As pretty as it was there, floating atop that organic masterpiece, I had no option but to float, for there was no method by which to drive the thing. As it was, the craft was lame, for want of an oar, a sail or some benevolent current. In the dead calm of that place, optionless, there was nothing but to wait in the wonder of it all. If I've learned one thing it was to wait, and not be tired by waiting.

It was then, just then, when I had deemed there no solution, that a curious radiance began to build in the bottom and very center of that lake. As the light's intensity grew, appearing as a great lamp arising from the depths, a sliver finally crested the waterline, quickly followed by a broadening arc, until it was the clear, it was a rising moon! Mid-lake!

The great and full sphere did not ascend on the traditional trajectory, but rather, vertically into the sky. Had I not known it to be impossible, I should have concluded that an army of men had fastened it to a cable of iron, made an astronomical pulley of Cassiopeia and were in concert to raise the great sphere aloft. For, the moon does not ascend from amidst the landscape, but from behind it. And, it does not ascend on an axis, such as was the case in view.

As the light created new visibility, I heard bubbling sounds of the water at my direct flank. When I turned to behold the disturbance, my eyes were met with a great boiling of the lake surface there. The sound was immediately behind me and when I looked to find the source of that water plume, expecting a great fish or the like, I was startled to find that a gentle geyser carried upon it, my cane spear emerging from those depths! I had resolved that I should never have seen that companion again, having cast it over the falls as I did. As I reached down to retrieve it from the surface, I was dawned by the realization that the spear was just the instrument to complete the enchanted punt. I could think nothing more prominently, than to think that I had thought that pike into existence once again. With the skill of a Venetian, I moved across the liquid painting of that lake, beneath that soaring moon. As if I had thought it into existence, as I struggled to think how I might move that punt along the sound, that spear proved just the lever I needed to guide the craft; moving through the canal of Venice.

As I retrieved that spike, happy to be reunited with my true companion, my left arm, if you will. Though, as I retrieved it, thinking of the miracle following into that place, it brought with it the pang of sorrow, which was that the jaguar had not appeared with it. For all that had happened in that strange relationship that had evolved between us, I felt an inexplicable melancholy for the loss of him; a sorrow for his drowning, as I imagined that such a death was worst of all for a cat. In the end, he was a nemesis because I feared him, but once that fear had dissolved and he was of no threat to me, I could see the good in him and the impact he had had on me.

Though it was with a pessimistic heart, I did wait for some time, staring into that Monet'ed surface, hoping to see his granite head surging from the deep. After some time, it became clear, my friend was lost to those waters forever. And then, I heard those voices again...that music which had led me to the place. There was none to do, but push forward in punt in search for that music's source

As I drifted through the landscape of that great reservoir, I did so with the great hope of human contact, as a way of returning home. I beached the punt and made haste for the gentle beach, someplace where that music was coming from. One final look out upon the lake, and to think of my lost companion therein..

With two sticks from the vegetation around me, I fashioned a makeshift grave-marker for the cat and plonk it into the shore. I had not been without my beaded jaguar vest since doffing it in that clearing, but it seemed the perfect marker for such a burial spot, as it had been for mine. I took a knee at the site, for a moment of gratitude and contemplation, and said goodbye to the jaguar.

With that, I made for the hedge of grasses behind me, in search of that nearby song...

CHAPTER 25

CHOSEN

y steps were not many, before I came upon the source of that magnificent music. I was discreted behind a fence of high grass, peering through the stripes of it, onto a most magnificent and sensual performance in the low waters at the shore. As fate deemed it, I became history's most fortunate voyeur, for in the shallows there, my eyes became drunk upon the view to a splendid assemblage of nymphets.

The cadre of bathing beauties numbered seven in all, none of whom appeared as indigenous to the Amazon, but rather, I surmise them Dutch. Six of them were magnificent younger women, all similar in age, each a near replica of the other: fair copies to an original masterpiece. Having described all the horrors and near death experiences within my adventure, how can I not stop briefly in this delicious pool, to share what I beheld upon my viewing of that aquatic flock?

They were women, young women, who were the result of a sculptor's care and longing. If they were not living creatures, I should have thought them cast from a stone far surpassing perfect marble, to some undiscovered variety that is born without blemish. The sextet initially appeared at water-play, but within minutes it was obvious they were deeply entranced, in some sort of ceremony. As their nubile trunks rolled in the shallows, over and around each other, they were each enrapt by a great length of vine. The slick vines appeared as the equivalent to sexual partners, so that their ecstatic writhing and moaning was not simple bathing, but some form of mating.

Their free spirited display allowed me to behold the wonder of their feminine prowess; the perfected combination of physical and mechanical beauty. They were delicious in their frolic. Initially, they lie horizontally, each upon her belly or back, making only the ripest places visible above the waterline. The interplay between their soft flesh and that quicksilvering water delivered a marvelous highlight upon their calves and crowns, their racks and rumps, until each island of flesh was, to my eyes, was a sifted dune upon The Arabian Sea.

Grangita III

Nothing, however, was equal to the moment each of them would become a-twist, elbows heather loft, entwined by those wet vines, and begin washing her own high back. It was in that perfect posture of the languid stretch, that wonderful valleys of shadow appeared in the deep clefts at the top of their ripe asses and between the blades of their bronzed shoulders. The scapula were so dramatically spread beneath the moonlight, that those darlings took the appearance of Titian butterflies at bath. Oh, if only to have been that soft moonlight, which fell upon the skin of them. For, it was that moonlight, which traveled over every part of every one of them, granted the unrestricted passage which belongs to moonlight alone.

As each reached and torsioned, the genesis of her beauty became evident, as the whole of her was so clearly organized about the dark and singular universe of her navel. The omphalic order to each completed nymph was the result of a first creative throw from each umbilic port. Their exquisite navels were elongated vertically, pulled into that erotic format by the tension between the elegant stretch of their shoulder beams and taught bellies.

Just beneath that nucleus of each one, appeared the wonderful suggestion of an anatomical bridge to be crossed, hidden just beneath their tawny flesh. The piers of those hidden trestles were long and pliant thighs, where the towers anchored therein, were soft pronounced hips at each extreme. To complete the dreamy structure, I imagined suspension cables, which draped the distance across their lower bellies, forming a delicate and inverted arch. As those hammocked lines of those imagined cables met with the loin-deck of each nymphet, they created an inverted brow above each perfect and grainless peach.

As if the physical ideal needed be italicized, each darling was crowned in cursive tresses, which were braided and trained over their polished shoulders. Those cascading plaits were sewn with every lovely meadow flower, so that they were equally woven to become fields of Buttonbush and Clover...as they were to become leas of Bluet and Tearthumb. While I remained in my hidden distance, the tiny feet of my imagination were quite happily lost, wandering through those hallowed, hairlined meadows.

Upon evidence in those bathing doves, were not the strokes of the sculptor's heavy pitching tools, but rather, the light touch of rifflers and emery stones...of time taken...of love given; evidence to the full quiver of one artist alone, who leaves no jag behind Him. At last, each lovely one appeared finished in iron oxide, which delivered them into that peerless and poreless copper hue. Those beloved were the perfect expression of softness and femininity and power in the mist that resides over such womanhood alone, which leaves a man's drenched lungs to clamor.

Juxtaposed against these six entranced nymphets, was a seventh. Unlike the sirens at her feet, the woman was enormous and earthy, and without question, she was of a significant age beyond them all. She was the physical counterpoint to those rollicking sprites, for she was so round as to be gelatinous, her flesh, deep and tumbling about her frame, as an oversized curtain. I suppose that I am saying, she was obese. But, to view her there, in her full glory as well, she was magnificent. In fact, amidst that entwined bevy, she made the others appear cliché. She generated such gravity upon my eyes that I could not have averted my attention, had I even wanted to do so. Her radiance and beauty bypassed reason, filling me with a wonderful sense of...abundance.

Only further dissolving my taste, the great heifer was smoking a cigar, which was on the scale of a jungle banana or a tobacco leaf. As decidedly unfeminine as the implement was, it only added to her coursing sensuality in some way. Even as desperate as my position had become, some involuntary channel in me, the carnal channel to be sure, was mesmerized to the point of an erection so powerful that it, too, was cast from a stone akin to marble, suddenly shrinking my loincloth to the point near breaking. She had officially turned my loins against my incumbent sensibilities.

As my erection and I observed her there, she had the carriage of a priestess or elder, strolling through that pond of those orgasmic pretties, blowing great pothers of smoke upon them as she passed. As the smoke, their writhing and the moaning commingled, the sexual energy in that river grew to a rolling boil. Between drags on that cheroot, the great woman revealed herself as that singular songstress, that artist behind the voice which had called to me from those high falls. While her tongue was foreign to me, the language she used had never been in my hearing, her voice proved so competent an instrument, so powerful, that her meaning was communicated perfectly. Her vocabulary of tone ranged widely, oscillating between the dulcet and the carnal, bespeaking a meditation upon gratitude, passion and pure hedonism. There was not least of turning in that voice. Every note from her throat, was a note of unapologizing truth.

Presently, the collected women's' expression was nearing a crescendo, as the mother of them then took to the shaking of a giant necklace of waita leaves, which generated the pitchy sound of maracas, elevating that fever of those girls to a fury. At last, the full pitch of their aggregated ecstasy, the priestess generated and held a single note so high and pure that it brought water to my eyes, and more importantly, it harmonized those six nymphets into a chorus. The synchronization of their physical expression turned them into a row of vibrating delights. Unwittingly, my attention so vested upon them, I had become harmonized to their vibration, as well, having begun a quiet moaning of my own. By the time I became aware that my volume was a threat to betray my covert status, it was too late for me to care. I had forgotten myself, past the point of no return, until I was finished by an involuntary and massive orgasm, leaving me in a loincloth steeped.

Within that moment of my ejaculation, inside the very denouement, the priestess', the older one, eyes flew open and fastened directly on my position behind those reeds. Her singing stopped sharply, her eyes cast into a distortedly wide position, and she breathed deeply through her nostrils, as if she could smell that musk that I had just released. Her fierce gaze upon my position melted position, behind those reeds behind which I sat, which was the end of my hiding. As she broke from that ecstatic state, so too did the six dove snap from theirs, becoming like a row of executioners awaiting the command to fire. Without exception, their adorable noses were skyward, eagerly collecting my scent, until, as a human cloud, the six naked nymphs surged to the priestess, literally balling themselves around her, until the large woman had become the centerpoint in a three dimensional collage of nudes. The sight was impossible enough to believe, but the strength of that priestess, who was standing easily under the weight of her clinging brood, was a feat beyond the sight itself. Only the priestess's eyes peered out through that human cloak, as the nymphets had gone into a state of humming wildly in agitation.

I rose from my grassy cover, tossing my cane spear to the side, as an act of complete surrender, announcing to them, "I come in peace. I mean you no harm."

Upon my leaving that cover and taking two or three steps toward them, the cloud of naked nymphs swarmed me, covering me in the same manner they previously covered their elder. There was no distinct difference in their assembly upon me, however, as every face of them organized itself about my manhood and their tongues darted as snakes, pulsing against the pouch of my loin cloth, where there was the fresh presence of my ejaculate. They were as a hive upon honey, so inflamed were they. As if there was time for the assessment of any kind, I discovered the trick behind the strength of that gelatinous priestess, for while I was covered by the buzzing six, they were nearly weightless upon me. Upon me, they each weighed nothing at all, as if they each were hollow at the core or made of some wondrous smoke. In any case, I was at their mercy, a happy prisoner ensnared by their wonderful flesh and stems.

The priestess then stepped forward to inspect me, beneath the full length cape of those beauties upon me. As she arrived, naked and free, she took a deep drag of that cigar she held between her great teeth, and began blowing smoke over the whole of me. That smoke, which I breathed in second hand, put me into an immediate state of surrender. It was not smoke in the traditional sense, but carried with it the weight of windswept silt. While the smoke nearly paralyzed me in relaxation, it did also have the benefit of calming that swarm which was upon me, so that their collective limbs and shanks allowed me some degree of restricted movement.

She then came upon me, surveying my body with her gentle finger, for the full length of me. Upon that contact, I swear it, as impossible as it seems, I was restored to a state of full arousal. Without the least refractory period from the mere minute before, my soldier was standing at full attention in the presence of command. The erection was even more powerful than the previous, so that my loin cloth finally gave way, falling comically to the earth. The heifer did all that with the touch of a single finger.

With the loss of my fig leaf, my shame was fully exposed, which sent those darlings into a frenzy, crawling about me as snakes in heat, anchored were they to my beam. The priestess knelt, her gorgeous mass heaving like a mountain of wax beneath me, then took a deep drag of her cheroot, finally blowing great clouds of that smoke upon my fully engorged manhood and into my ass. She then hungrily dove into the smoke, bringing her fleshy face into such a proximity as to fellate me, and then danced her tongue about the head of my cock, taking a draft of the semen thereon. While she did this, I had the most curious feeling of her magic finger making way into the port of my ass. Upon this recall, I would like to believe that she had paralyze me with that smoke, leaving me unable to resist that assholed finger, but the truth of it was: I loved it. Whatever she was doing to me, she owned me completely.

She appeared to direct the swarm upon me, with her eyes, so that the women began adjusting their positions. One of them relieved the priestess from the massaging of my prostate, which was like a changing of the guards. The priestess then rose to look me in the eyes, her lovely breath upon my face, and took my great cock into the counsel of her right hand. She began massaging it, pulling it backward, as to tighten the helm. I couldn't be sure what her intention was to search to satisfy or to slay, but unable to control myself, I finished again, into her hand. The women upon me were in a fury at that scent, all eager...desert horses gathered 'round a watering hole. The priestess gave the collected women a look with her eyes and they surged upon my manhood, sniffing, licking and otherwise, until they had quite finished with me. As quickly as they had come upon me, they then dismounted as a swarm and stood in rank behind their gelatinous queen.

The priestess spoke, "You have no barb."

"I'm sorry? No barb?"

"How did you come upon this place, savage?"

"It will sound to you, the ramblings of a fool, I'm afraid."

"How did you come upon this place, savage?"

"I came over a great waterfall. I was plunged into the depths beneath it and upon my finding its floor, I was then pulled by a deep current, through a natural tunnel thereunder, until I did surface in this very lagoon."

She was nonplussed, continuing her inquiry, "Savage, tell me this: Were you pursued over these falls into this place?"

"Followed, you mean? Was I followed?"

"Not followed. Pursued."

"I was, in fact, pursued. Though, I don't know if I was followed. I think not."

"And this pursuer...? Tell me of this pursuer."

"It was a great cat. It was, is, was, is…was a magnificent, black jaguar with amber eyes."

I shared, my affection for the cat, unrestrained.

Upon mention of the cat, her eyes registered some excitement or meaning or significance, as did the row of maids behind her, who stood at attention.

"You have no barb. You have been brought here upon the back of a jaguar."

"Yes, ma'am, on the back of the cat. He plunged with me, over these falls, but I have not seen him since. I believe…I believe he has drowned in these waters. For, I have not seen him."

The woman moved forward to me, studying my eyes deeply, in search of a lie, I suppose. Seemingly satisfied, she stepped back from me briefly, and from around her neck, she lifted a small skull. When she raised the skull before me, I discovered it featured two long horns, which were actually formed by two straws emerging from the temples on forty five degree angles. She carried a small pouch at her side, inside of which was revealed a dark brown and black powder of some kind. With great intention, she packed one of the straws, as if loading a rifle. She then inserted that packed straw into her nose and inserted the other straw into her mouth, so that the skull was the apex between the two. She then blew with great force from her mouth, which produced a loud whoosh, as the powder that occupied that straw was sent hurtling into her nostril. As she removed the implement, there was a tardy cloud of ash that dissipated from around the rim of her nose.

She repeated this procedure into the opposite nostril, as well. In reaction, her eyes grew wide briefly, as if she had snorted some black species of cocaine.

"It had been said, that there is one who will come..." she spoke as she was administering the substance to her maids, each having the blow rifled into their sinuses by her. Each coughing out the residual, which clearly traveled the bypass between nose and pallet. She continued, "This one who has been promised, he is one who is triune: warrior, poet and mate."

She then approached me, loading that skull apparatus, so that my growing concern was making me deaf to her speaking.

"This one of the prophecy, will come on the back of a cat... and will have no barb upon his manhood..."

She stuck one end of the straw end into my nostril and I was frozen in her trance. She blew fiercely into the other end of the straw, sending a single blast of that powder through my nose, brain tissue and, I was certain, to the back of my very skull. Just beyond the initial searing of it, as if a pick had been sent through the center of my head, I was quickly attended by the feeling of total clarity and well-being.

"Look to the lake, savage. What do you see there, high, high above it?"

"There is a moon, which has risen from the center of the lake, still dripping itself dry there. I saw it rise, upon my arrival to the place. It ascended vertically, as if upon a chain that hoisted it thusly."

"And this one who is promised...this one who may come... he will bring with him, a blood moon." she spoke, inserting the straw into my other nostril.

"He of the prophecy, is one like you, who meets these three requirements. Close your eyes, Savage."

I did as instructed and last I knew, I felt another of those ashen rifle balls moving through the port of my nostril and into the back of my head...

𝕭𝕴𝕹𝕲𝕰

CHAPTER 26

THE UNFINISHED SKY

h, the luxurious feeling began at the very top of my head and was unbroken the length of me, right down to the soft, parabolic arch around my every toe. Oh, how every muscle within the duffel of my skin was completely at rest, the wonderful weight of sand in a sock. My skin was a tingle, as every pore upon me was being attended by its own champagning bubble; a million carbonated chaperones, scrubbing clean the every cell of me.

My eyes were closed, so happily closed, and I had no ambition to open them, preferring instead to ingest my surroundings by way of alternative and much preferred senses. I was at rest in a small body of water, which rocked and floated the weight of me, heaving me gently in a hundred directions, as the lowly waters echoed between the walls of my bath and the lead of myself.

There is nothing to compare to the sound of bath water amidst an otherwise silence. It has the unique character of smuggling within itself, its own reiteration, which is what gives it that exquisite three dimensional sound. It is so heavenly when limbs emerge from beneath the surface and hovers just above the waterline, releasing from them a trickle, producing that wonderful tapering signature…the sound that bath water alone will make.

I was, as well, ensconced in the wonder of a nude chaise at my back. Her fingers were long and delicate reeds, each digit a soloist, waltzing the parquet of my skull. Her pattern was disciplined, traveling the sequence from my crown, drifting down the hollows at my temples and retiring to the shade of my posterior skull. Over and over again, she repeated this figure, releasing every headly tension therein. Of course, that luxury was deepened by symmetry, as another bathing companion was at the opposite end of me, involved in the same enterprise of massage, working with keen insistence beneath the arches of my feet.

I opened my eyes slowly and thankfully, to discover my great tub and its wonderful nymphets. Ravishing, were they, nude and partially submerged, made only more so by a third who was sitting faithfully tub-side, holding a wonderful cup of tea for me. As I rolled my heavy head to her, she brought the cup to my lips, where I could reach to draft of it. Floating atop the surface of that tea were cloves and scalloped wild mushrooms, which had been so steeped as to become translucent. The pekoe tasted superb, but even greater did it become, as it landed on the hub inside my center chest, from which it was distributed outward through me, delivering upon it the feeling of the deepest well-being. Of course, what would a great tea be, without a nude maiden to produce one of those small skulls about her neck, so as to blast the nostrils of my companions and me with that wonderful nose candy. The combined effect of the tea and that mystery powder created the beautiful first flush of entering the doorway to drunkenness, where Heat and Tingle move like friendly soldiers delivering their unique rations.

Maybe I had become a wee stoned, but the tub itself was positively mesmerizing, in both its scale and fabrication. The three of us fit quite comfortably within it and I dare say there was room for several more of them. Oh, dear God, thought I, please, several more of them. It was a pedestal basin, sitting in the middle of a jungle hut, into which was streaming tree filtered moonlight through windows upon every side of it. The great body of the vessel was copper, which had been fabricated under a thousand lashings of Punraz' hammer. Each dented strike created its own small recess, until it was a ball-peened master work. In contrast to those myriad strikes upon the skin, the lip around the edge rolled fatly, making it the perfect form over which to drape my surrendered limbs. Adding to its one of a kind appearance, the skin bore a unique signature of age upon copper, which is to say that it was covered in a creeping abstract of patina. Upon its clawed feet and given that turquoise marking over the flesh of it, it's body gave the appearance of a copper giraffe or brass leopard.

Perhaps my high and the context exaggerated the light and color, but those thousands dents in the surface, combined with the brilliance of the copper, distributed the ambient moonlight in every direction, until that light had painted the whole of that hut as a universe unto itself.

Magnificent was the tub; curious was the water. The water therein was not water, at all, but a combination of ingredients, which made it more akin to a white soup. The watery substance was colored as milk, which pigment had come to paint we three in tub, so that we were covered in a hueless white. The only color upon my companions was produced by their hair, the flowers woven into their braids and their lovely eyes. The same could be said of me, for every inch I could see was painted in that blanche.

Additionally, the water was littered with plants and spices, so that we were being steeped in a medicinal melange. The smells of it was healing variety, heavily laden with aromatics, such as menthol and tea tree oil... patchouli and clove. The fragrance had a heat and piercing-ness to it, which did yeoman's work in opening the sinuses as well as sustaining that tingle over the whole of me. Present in the midst of those spices, was floating one of those striking vines, which I had seen those darlings entwined at the shore.

In addition to my three attendants at tub, the remaining three were busily grinding dried flower petals within small stone basins, as squaws reducing maize to flour. Just behind them I caught sight through one of those windows, to the surrounding creation. Upon my view through it, I could see that we were engulfed in a network of great limbs and branches, which based on their size and character, were centuries old. We were clearly in a house high up and within a tree.

My attending nubiles then coaxed me to stand up in the tub, which I did. Each took a position, one at my fore, one at the aft, each upon her knees. My manhood was at complete rest, as a retired pendulum before that genuflect nymphet. While I stared down upon her, our positions suggesting an impending liaison, she lifted her hands from beneath the water, revealing my dagger in her closed fist! Erotic ambitions retreated, as did my startled cock, but expression and motions were such that she communicated no intended harm to come. She hushed me and indicated that I should be perfectly still and surrender to them, which I did.

The one at my aft was lathering me with some wonderful salve, and I was awash in foam which smelled of cocoa butter and menthol. The be-daggered darling then began to work from the top of me, shaving my skull with that single blade. She worked with the skill of a barber, the blade deftly tracing the entirety of my head, including the removal of my eyebrows and beard alike. Her blade traveled with purpose down the length of me, removing any remnant of hair left upon me. My anxieties began welling, as I could see that there was a flight path to the prominent bush about my manhood and into the dim places beneath my scrotum. Breathlessly, I watched, not moving a centimeter, as the fuller and tip of that great knife danced around my cock and balls, without incident. As I was recovering my breath, she was already making final work of the taper to my ankles. At last, I stood in that copper bath, completely hairless, that white paint then drying upon me, until it had become a thinly glaze.

The others then rose from their positions at the adjacent table, bringing with them, the basins of powder which they had been grinding, in addition to a large yellow gourd. When they arrived to my station, I could see into each of the stone cups was an array of powdered pigments, which represented a pallet of brilliant colors. As the nudes patted me dry with grainless silks, I felt like a god. The seven of us, naked in a that high hut, far above the earth, and me, as the very Sun, about which those lovely planets were in orbit.

One of them inverted the gourd over the top of me, sending an oleaginous slick over the length of me. As the oil traveled leisurely from my crown to my feet, the darlings hummed in unison, as the seraphim of Isaiah, working diligent to baste me with their exquisite hands. At last, I stood anointed, as a glycerined albino.

They had put me into a state of such repose and wonder, that I admit I asked them no questions, nor did I resist their keen enterprise. Next I knew, they began a lengthy process of applying those pigmented powders upon me. Their keen focus and dancing brushes, stroked me as masters animating an empty canvass. The ceremony went on for hours, until at last the synchronized six stepped back to assess the work they had completed. They were positively a twitter, exceedingly satisfied with their output. I, of course, could not gain the comprehensive view, as they. I could only see by way of a downcast aspect, that the primary hues upon me were far from that albino tarp, which had covered me at the start.

The one who had shaved me with the great blade, retrieved the instrument for me. I held the dagger's chaste silver blade aloft before me, finding that it provided a wonderful surrogate for a mirror. As I studied my reflection in the tapered speculum, I was astounded to find that they had painted me as a canvass of the night sky. I was awash in magnificent, deep blues and blacks.. indigos and aquamarines. The great drifts of vaporous whites, which traveled across me as dandelion matter, represented star filled clusters. The mural was so realistic and comprehensive, that there was no trace left of me, save my gaping eyes.

"It is marvelous, my darlings." said I.

They giggled and nodded in response, so happy were they with their output.

BINGE

"Can you tell me, what all of this is about?" I asked.

"It is for Pachamama to say." they responded in perfect unison.

"I'm afraid you have forgotten something here. Where is the moon? Have you hidden it upon my back?"

"It is for Pachamama to say." they responded in perfect unison.

One of them then took the empty gourd, from which that oil had been poured, and submerged it into the earthy brew of that copper tub. Handing it to me, they said in unison, "Drink this, savage."

"What is it?"

"Drink it please." they insisted gently.

"You must tell me what all of this is for?" I responded.

"You will see, savage. Pachamama will show you. Now you must drink."

"Pachamama?"

"Yes."

"Who is she? The one from before? Your queen?"

"Our Mother."

"You are all her children?"

"We are each her children, but we are not all her children. Pachamama is the mother to the flower...to the creature in the garden...and, to us, too. All belongs to Pachamama. Drink now, savage. No more questions."

She lifted the gourd to my lips and of that bath water, I drank.

BINGE

CHAPTER 27

ORIONIS

he sextet led me from the hut, then a long staircase, which helixed 'round the trunk of the Samaúma tree, which stood at fifty meters high and must have been five hundred years in the growing. As we descended, a cloud of villagers was collecting at the bowl of the tree, where it's chiseled calves met with the rich, dark earth in which it stood. All those eyes cast upward, should have caused more concern in me, for I was still naked and at that immodest angle to them. Factors putting me at ease, however, included the dense cloak of that paint over the whole of me AND the dawning discovery in my descent, that every other villager was completely naked, as well. As my maidens and I arrived at the base, I moved with the ease of a gigolo from the last riser into that adoring throng.

As I was greeted by the general population of the colony, I discovered another heavenly fact, which may have been the only such fact, which could have made their practice of corporate nudity even greater. Specifically, within that great swarm of villagers, which numbered in the thousands, there was not another man to be seen. As best I could tell, I was the sole toto there in their village, which awareness was only pressed more keenly upon me, by those thousands of dancing eyes, upon the spectre of my indigoed manhood. I moved like a parade elephant through the village, escorted on all sides by conjugal trainers, my trunk leading the procession, swinging clumsily from side to side.

The procession, however, would come to take on the full flavor of an emperor's arrival into a great city, as I was delivered BY them on a wonderfully ornamented litter. The celestial construct was in the ancient tradition of the royal sedan chair, featuring two long poles at each side, which allowed for the vessel to be shouldered by slaves. Rather than a seat, however, the platform upon which I would ride, was a luxurious bed, teeming with the most exotic white fabrics, each of some impossible thread count. The length of the opulent skiff was proportioned as a traditional bed, where the headboard was of a higher cast than the foot, so that the profile of the thing took on the full character of a crescent moon, upon its back. About the base of it, beneath that recumbent moon, the outfacing bed rails were composed of a row of symmetrical skulls, which performed as a grim wainscoting. And, so as not risk the least chance of understatement, the hedonistic float was unified by handles which were shaped as inordinate phalluses, both ends of which were helmed.

𝕭𝖎𝖓𝖌𝖊

As I climbed upon it, there was no way to orient myself, but to lay extended and languid upon it, so that my posture was involuntarily erotic. My amaranthine pigment, stood out prominently against the dark monochrome of those white fabrics, until I must have appeared toward all gathered, as a sapphire sheep upon a snow drift. I would have been nourished the way, as waiting for me, upon the craft, were a collection of divine fruits. Omitted were the likes of dull candidates, such as the tiresome apple, the pasty banana or worst of all, the droll pear. Favored within that great tureen, were the romantic yield— peaches, plums, strawberries and grapes—of which every part was erotically shaped and edible, the lot of which exploded upon contact with the eager mouth. As I rode and et, my chin became slicked in the sweet overflow of those sensual fruits.

As the women lifted me into the air with ease, to their collective shoulder height, I was floating upon a bronzed sea, wherein the cresting waves were the copper shoulders and the troughs between them, taught, russet shanks. I admit I became so lost in the headiness and luxury of it, that I even came to imagine their jungle percussion having been replaced instead by the sounds of French horns, kettle drums and cymbals.

The royal litter is, to my taste, the single greatest mode of transport extant, far outperforming a man's crusted soles upon a jungle floor or his harrowing flight from precipitous waterfall or cliff.As I floated upon that feminine tide, I admit I wished it had been longer than those hundred steps or so. But, alas, we had arrived to some transcendent garden gate, which was our destination.

The great throng grew immediately still and perfectly quiet, which cast that moment and place into a sudden...sacredness. All of those lovely creatures had fallen to their knees, so that as I stood at that considerable gate, above them all, their collective penitence had turned them into landscape of headless boulders, earthed the way to the horizon far behind me.

The gate itself was equally ominous and wondrous, which character was only amplified by the behavior of that prostrate company. It was not a gate of iron, but rather, it was of a naturally occurring construct, the result of collaborating trees and vines. The great portal was in the format of pishtaq, that far eastern shape, which is so singular, appearing as the spade one finds upon that black suit of cards. Those towering plants, which formed its mysterious character, appeared to me as lovers embracing over a fence, where they were each anchored firmly within the opposing sides of the path, but bent happily at the high waist, so as to fulfill their entwining ambitions. Just inside, the interior corridor disappeared around the soft corner, making the way for a lovely mystery and the draw to discover it, irresistible.

I lifted the fallen face of my maid, the one who carried my dagger and cane spear, and asked, "Will you be coming with me, my darlings?"

In reverence, she offered, "None can pass through that gate, but you. Beyond that gate is only for Pachamama and the one who is called."

"My sweet nymphs, what awaits me in this place?"

"We cannot answer for we do not know. It is for Pachamama to say."

I was going to enter. I knew that I had to enter, and yet I further questioned her as some tactic or delay, "Who has entered this gate before?"

"None has entered before you, savage."

A breeze emerged from that enchanting corridor, drifting over the gathered there, upon which travelled that remarkable voice, which was that of Pachamama, the queen.

The nymph then rose and handed me my great dagger and my cane spear, which I gently took from her. "I thank you, each. The way for me is clear, but you have made this leg of my journey...the way of love and kindness. I shall not forget you, any."

"She calls you now, savage. There is only to go to her. For she believes it is of you, that this has been written."

She fell to her face again, as the rest and I turned to make way into the place, sorrow-filled, leaving that band of nymphets behind. The path beneath my feet took long, soft turns and after a few hundred strides and several curves of that lane, the world of that village and its people was completely gone from my reference. With every step I took, that world I had just left, disappeared, to such a degree, that I questioned it as some sort of dream. Were it not for those pigments o'er the flesh of me, I should have thought them each imagined, so immediately ensconced was I in the wonder of that emerging place.

I arrived to a place, or better said, the place, which was a magnificent garden. I say it was a garden, which is to differentiate it from the wild and unkempt jungle, as a place which was the result of great care and intention and love. The result of a romance between man and nature.

The garden was of a scale that was positively breath taking, organized by some sacred geometry, which produced a harmony within and between every plane of it. Long, symmetrical walkways of decomposed granite ran like arteries through seeming endless hedges and towers of trumpeting flowers. Natural fountains and falls whispered throughout the landscape and those mighty trees acted as nature's anchors, stretching their eager tentacles to the banks of nearby streams. Flowers and vegetables were growing in pedicured rows, which stretched tastefully in all directions from a center point. All that was displayed there was perfectly complimented by the perfumed air, which had been engineered, no doubt, so that to walk through that garden was to walk through the sheer veil of heaven itself.

At the very epicenter of all that vitality, I discovered her, kneeling upon the ground, before a swath of vigorous herbs and spices. She was every bit that earthy, Rebenesque beauty, made all the more so by that great cigar she kept clenched between her teeth. She appeared at a worship, which I threatened to interrupt, singing to those plants and blowing clouds smoke upon them. As soon as she detected my presence, she rose to greet me, inventorying the length of me with her sage eyes.

"I see my nymphs have done a splendid work in rendering you thus. You are positively...majestic."

CHAPTER 28

CONSTELLATING

he was so familiar in her way with me, as if we'd known each other a lifetime. She welcomed me in the tradition of the East, hands together in the manner of prayer and bowing. I clumsily followed her lead and she wove one of her great arms into mine, setting us out in the garden in the way of a husband and wife.

"Let us walk this path together, savage. We have only this time to prepare, which is this single walk upon this single path in this single direction, yes?"

"I am yours, Pachamama. It is my privilege to take this walk with you."

Contact with her drove me mad with lust, which I could not negotiate. There was no explaining that power that she had, other than to say that standing in her physical presence was like being in a field of pure sexual energy. When I was within that radius, interlocked with her, my body was no longer my own, as had been indicated by another of those mammoth erections.

"Ah, yes, it is wonderful to see such a fine cock in this garden." she said, matter of factly.

"My apologies, Pachamama, but I have no control over my body, when I am near you." I explained.

Genuinely perplexed by my answer she responded, "You apologize for this energy between us? When your body speaks the truth of a wonderful possibility, should you apologize for that truth? Do you imagine me unhappy to have this affect upon you?"

"I...I don't know." I admit, I was so stunned by such clear reasoning, as the way she had put it to me, made me feel more foolish for my apology than my post.

"With all we will face this night, you must let go these judgements you carry. Truth alone lives in this garden. If it is true, then it is right. Surrender your mind to this place, savage, as you walk with me."

Her manner in was so calming and straight forward. There was not the slightest of shame or pride or falseness in her. Whether it was in the way she spoke or moved, she was this lovely weave of acceptance and honesty... and love. That greatness both inspired me and made me aware my unworthiness of mind, while I was in her presence.

"You say, that we face something great this night. I don't know what is expected of me, but you must know that I am a man very much lost in this jungle, not only to the place, but to almost every memory of who I am."

She smiled, registering the hearing of me, but was clearly more interested in the feel of ferns, through which she dragged her easy hand.

"Is it not so wonderful to be this one man, unburdened?"

"Unburdened?" I said, slightly indignant.

"Ah, forgetting is amongst the greatest gifts we have of the mind. It is always forgetting, which allows two people to live inside a single moment together, at peace. Only forgetting has this pleasant power."

The ease with which she spoke and the paradox within the truth themselves was doing a great work in disarming me. Though what she said seemed the absolute truth of things, I found a default resistance in my mind. "You have an optimistic outlook on this amnesia, which I suffer." I challenged.

She reached to a lovely, yellow flower, plucking it from its stem, breathing it deeply in and then offered it to me.

"Do you suffer, savage? Are you not very much alive in this moment with this yellow flower and me? Is there something greater you wish, than to be loved and alive, as you are in this very moment?"

Ohhhh, the sweet smell of that flower was someplace deep in my recall. And, though I knew nothing of plants, I knew that single bloom to be the Carolina Jessamine. The perfume of that flower, delivered a wonderful spring of joy thorough me.

"The way you say things to me, Pachamama, I know that you speak truth, and yet, this truth I resist. I admit that I am free, as you say, but I am also betrayed by some compulsion to recover the memory of who I am...where I have come from... to where I will return."

"I can help you in this, my darling savage." She swept her arm with wide view to the lush place around us, saying, "You are this man who walks with me in this garden. You have just come from that stride behind us and you are now here. You are free to go as you wish from this place we stand, yes?"

"Is it really as simple as you say, Pachamama?"

"It is and it isn't." she said thoughtfully. "The truth is simple, but accepting it, is often difficult.

"Your way, Pachamama, is the way of truth and kindness, I know it. If I say, as that ancient man has said before me, 'I believe, Pachamama, but help me in my unbelief', will you do it for me?"

"I am happy in this moment with you, that this need in you can be met by this part of me. That is what we must be to each other, savage. For it is we together, who must do this thing tonight."

"Pachamama, you say again, of this night, there is something we must do. Has this to do with why I have been rendered as a night sky?"

"Yes. You are donning the camouflage of heaven. But, you are not merely a night sky. You are most important part of the heavens on this night. Do you not recognize yourself, as you are?"

"I have seen myself only in the slender mirror that is my own dagger. I have seen that I am this night sky with stars cast upon it. That is what I have seen."

"You see with eyes that are not your own. So deep is your blindness, that while you cannot remember your very self, you cannot forget this blindness."

"Have I not described the truth of these images upon me?"

"You have described what you have seen, savage, but you have not yet perceived."

"Will you help me, Pachamama? I want to understand, not merely to see."

"There are things which are written upon us, which we have not learned, but were given to us, each. A truth, which is written upon our hearts."

"And you believe I possess such knowledge? Knowledge, which is not acquired, but which has been with me?"

"I know you have. For this knowledge of you, is the knowledge, which has written upon me. Look to your right shoulder, savage…tell me what you see there?"

I did as she asked and responded, "There is a yellow star there, of some size."

"You know this star. For, you know every star within the heavens, for that is your inheritance that is upon your heart. Name this star, which you know."

I took to the manner of deep thinking, though nothing occurred to me, as she believed it would. I was frustrated, but also embarrassed. I so wanted to please her AND to believe that she spoke a profound truth to me.

She took my face into her hands, and encouraged me, "You are stuck in this thinking. When you think, you are a man who is searching for a treasure within the shallow waters of a stream. Your agitation is what clouds these waters and hides this treasure you seek. Be still, your mind, and trust, so that these waters may settle."

It was impossible for me to let go of thinking, when it was that of which I was asked to do.

She drew her face closer to mine, so that her sweet breath was upon my very face. "Look at my wet lips, great man, and taste of this honey, which drips from my mouth for you alone."

I leaned in hungrily, dissolved into her wet mouth, lost in the sweet taste of a thousand summer fruits.

I suddenly pulled back and blurted out, "Betelgeuse. This star upon my shoulder, is Betelgeuse."

She was pleased with my recall. "You see, you are the warrior, but some other the questions, which the poet alone can answer. You cannot take a thought by force, as some animal you hunt."

"Indeed. And if such a kiss from you is the solution to this blindness I suffer, I shall wish this blindness for yet another lifetime."

"You see, how you are the poet, too. With the knowledge of that single star, you will now orient yourself. Let me help you."

She put her delicious finger into that yellow star at my right shoulder and with her opposite hand she reached down to my left knee and touched me there, such that her cheek was bushing against the steel of my disobedient cock.

"Close your eyes, as I will touch these stars, and you will come to recognize yourself by my touch."

I did as she suggested, which amplified her heat upon my body.

"You know by the distance from this one star from the other upon your knee. Feel my touch upon your flesh and trust that is written."

"This star is Rigel..." I said without thinking.

She then made contact with the opposite knee, her head and lips drifting over the landscape of my loins, as she passed.

"Saiph..." I uttered, as a voice, which was behind my own, was speaking to her.

Her full lips and tongue were slippery and surrendered, as they made passage over the shaft of my pulsing dome, arriving to the cavern of my navel, where her tongue dove into the marvelous darkness there. "It is the Trapezium Cluster, my darling, which your tongue is now drifting through."

Her fingers then danced repeatedly over three spots across my waist, just above my navel, until I trembling, spoke, "Alnitak, Alnilam and Mintaka."

She was a-fever, her voice like smoke, as she moaned and ascended. "Mmmm...you're delicious, my love. You are very well, indeed."

She kissed a hundred tiny steps from that row of stars, upon the trunk of me, her great ride of hair brushing against my face, as she arrived to my left shoulder, which she sucked and sucked and sucked upon.

"The star is Meissa, upon the round of my left shoulder!"

I was in the full pitch of lust, for she was such a teacher as that. I was overcome, and dove hungrily into her great mouth, as her pink tongue traveled freely within my hunger. My hands were wild and roaming over the mass of her, until the two of us were writhing upright. I spun her 'round, so that I was behind her, as a beast, my hands traveling her desperately, and I then buried my face into her great neck. She was yielding, as I reached down to discover my first contact with her slick vajeen, but with a sudden power of her arms, she arrested me, snapping us both from that trance.

"No. We mustn't, savage! We are too close, now. There will be this moment, but first, we face this test. We cannot risk this now."

"There is no risk, but the unexpressed passion like this." I pleaded.

"The risk is death itself, savage. You will see, when it is revealed to you. It is death for us, which may be waiting. This night is too important and we must wait to discover this good thing between us."

I was dizzy, so breathless had I become. "I will trust what you say is true, as I have trusted this knowledge you have revealed within me."

"Now is the time, my darling. These stars have revealed a portrait to you, yes?"

"I would say to you, Pachamama, that these stars have formed the figure of a great constellation, but, for the want of a single star to complete it, which is not present."

"Yes, that is my darling savage. You are right to say that one single star will reveal the final truth of you. This star you will only find, when you assume the position to which you have been called this night."

With that from her, I anchored my stony feet into a powerful base beneath me. I twisted my torso as a modest corkscrew above my knees and my right arm cocked behind me, as if pulling back the immense bowstring. And, at last, I extended the iron of my left arm to complete the singular starry tableau. Hidden, just there, within the crease at my left pectoral and shoulder, was revealed that final star, which completed the portrait upon me!

"The final star is Bellatrix, my love, and I am none other than The Great Hunter, Orion!"

CHAPTER 29

THE MOON

achamama was holding my hand and leading, her pace dramatically quickened, as her keen eyes were focused to the sky, in pursuit of some high demon. Upon the revelation, which was the heavenly costume, her gait and demeanor had transitioned from relaxed to frantic.

"Why do we now hurry, my love?"

"Look to the heavens, savage! It has begun! This time for us is passing quickly!" She was breathing heavily, the combination of her mood and pace.

As I cast my eyes upon that night sky, there was that great spill of stars in all directions. The sequined blanket of the eventide was only more brilliant, aided by the jungle's darkness. The density of that bespangled canopy, made obvious, one great void above our position. A hole in those heavens. Within an instant, I realized what had been omitted from the place.

"My love, he is gone this night from the heavens!"

"Yes, but he with me in this garden, now. It must be finished upon this night, Orion, or never!"

"I am not merely painted as he?!"

"One night beneath this unfinished sky is all there will ever be, for it is this night alone, upon which this thing must be finished."

She came to a sudden stop, her expression blanched, as she registered view of the heavenly object she pursued.

"You see now, savage! The hunt has begun!"

The ease of her face was lost, replaced by desperation, as she pointed to the oversized moon above.

"I can see this full moon, Pachamama. What is it that has so o'ertaken you? What is this hunt?"

"It is not the full moon that you see, but look closer, while it is disappearing before our very eyes."

As I looked again, there was the slightest degree of crescent shadow, which had appeared as a mascara upon the lunar-face.

"Is this moon in eclipse tonight?" I asked.

"This night alone will deliver The Blood Moon, which makes possible the task before us."

We dashed another fifty meters or so, into that waning orb, until, at last, we came into the spectre of a magnificent silhouette against the creole sky. There before us, was a tree of such majesty and scale that upon the very sight of it, my bowels turned to water. It was a tower stretching so far into the celestial sphere that to view its crown was impossible, appearing to break the floor of heaven itself. As the variegations in the stupendous canopy filtered the flood of moonlight, the effulgence fell to the earth as stoutly arrows, which plunged into the lush fabric of earth, which was the sacred ground about that tree. As that moonlight spilled, it also made translucent the individual leaves over the branches of it, turning electric, that umbrageous parasol. At last, the great plume of that tree appeared pulsing.

As I stood agape and dwarfed, a sturdy breeze passed suddenly through the heights of it, rattling that great foliole umbrella. Upon that wind, were loosed thousands of leaflets from that tree, and they came falling to earth as a drift of hazel snowflakes. As we stood amidst that impromptu fall, the myriad leaves carried the midnight's glimmer, to which Yeats pledged such deep affection.

I looked to Pachamama, her face in the carriage of profound sorrow. She bent over to pick up one of the fallen leaves, then revealing a stream of tears upon her cheeks.

"What of these leaves has upset you, so?" I asked gently.

"These are not leaves, which fall." she spoke gravely.

She held out an open palm for me, so that I could see what she held was some form of tiny pod. The pod was rocking in her open palm, until, at last, it slowed and then stopped.

"This shower upon us, is a shower of the dead, which comes in these times, even under the slightest breeze."

"A shower of the dead? These pods are but dying leaves. And the leaves on this tree are endless. There must be thousands to replace these fallen few."

She then directed her attention to the stream, which ran beside us in the distance, behind that tree.

"Look, too, at this stream which runs beside us. What do you see?"

"It is lovely in this waning moonlight. The water moves like mercury."

"But, it is not the river, which tells the story of the stream. It is the banks, alone, which speak of waters past."

"These high banks are lovely, too. But, will you tell me what I am not seeing?"

"These banks have become too tall and the river, too short between them"

"This river, it is dying?"

"It is."

"Rivers die. Rivers move. This is as it should be, no?"

"If it were another river, perhaps. But, this is a river that must never die, for it is this river that provides the consciousness of every living thing."

"You mean this water carries some form of consciousness upon it?"

"This stream that runs before you IS consciousness. This river alone feeds this tree, which slowly dies above us."

"What tree is this, Pachamama?"

"This is The Tree of Life, which must be saved. It is not the leaf which grows upon these branches, but the chrysalis. Within each like this one, there is a soul imbued with consciousness, by that stream alone. It is from this tree that every soul will come, whether creature, plant or man."

"My love, tell me what must be done this night, and I will make it so."

"There is but one way to restore this river, but it will be the act of him whose consciousness is equal to the calling. He will be the warrior, the poet and the mate. I believe you are these things, savage."

"Can you be certain?"

"You will either succeed in this hunt or you will not. If you fail, we shall perish. If you succeed, so shall we live."

We had arrived at a collection of natural fencing, amidst which was a stony staircase, which disappeared into a density of vegetation. There, at that entrance, was a small cauldron, remarkably like the one I had seen in the clearing from which I so narrowly escaped. The cistern was boiling with some dark and rancid brew. Additionally, as a table had been set, my cane spear and dagger, awaiting my arrival.

"Tell me what must I do, my queen, to finish this thing for you?"

"Savage, you must bring me the moon this night."

"The moon?!" I reacted in horror. "That is impossible!"

"And yet, it must be done...tonight. The Blood Moon alone is what you must hunt and bring to me in this garden, Orion."

"Pachamama, you cannot be serious! If it is the moon you require, no man, called or otherwise, can bring you this treasure. As my heart is pure and bursting to satisfy you, it just cannot be done."

"The one who is promised, is the one who can bring this thing. You are the shepherd of the heavens, Orion. This man is you, who wears the camouflage. But, you must raise your consciousness to meet this moment."

"I see that you are sincere, but I think you may be mad in this request. Whether one night to hunt this moon, or a thousand."

"Remember, the man who searches for the treasure in the stream. This man must be still, to make those waters clear. Don't think. You must trust that this answer has been written upon your heart."

She retrieved the wooden cup from near the cauldron, then dipping it into that steeping brew.

"You must take this. Drink it when you arrive at the dark lake's shore. Do not hesitate in doing this, for it will make possible the consciousness you need."

" What is this drink you have made for me?"

"It is the product of those vines, which you first discovered my nymphs entangled with, at the low waters of the shore. This, too, is the water, steeped in that copper tub with you. This is Ayahuasca you will drink, which will make visible what is otherwise hid from you."

"Am I granted any other tool but this dagger and cane spear of mine? Is there no instrument...no manual to aid me?"

"I can give you only this drink, but also warn you. If you are not him who is called, if I am wrong this night, you will have drunk your death."

"But if I am he who has been chosen...?"

"Then you will bring me this captured moon."

"Then I fear not, to draught of this and die. I fear only that I might fail you in capturing this Blood Moon, my love. I would prefer to drink my death than to return, empty handed."

"You will not fail. I know that you will not fail."

"If I survive this night, will you be waiting for me? Tell me this is so, and I will do this impossible thing for your love and love alone."

"I will be abed within the bowl of this great tree, when you will bring me this moon. And you alone shall drink of my cup and taste of this flesh, which will be yours alone."

"Where then?"

"Ascend these stairs, from my garden, which call to your feet alone, Orion. You will be shortly come upon the black lake, which awaits you. There, you will face what you must face...and alone. Go now and fail me not!"

Upon her command, I quickly ascended, armed with the wooden vessel, cane spear and that inherited dagger. As I dissolved into my waiting destiny, I did so in the blue-black camouflage of heaven.

CHAPTER 30

MOON HUNT

arrived to the clearing, where I was met by the brief shore of a black pond. The lagoon was impossibly secluded, hedged in all directions by a great density of growth, which featured all manner of vegetation, vine, and most prominently, towering trees, which stood as pickets against the night sky. The effect of that thickening and the bleak of water, worked to deliver the setting into a profound silence. Sound was crippled there by the muffle of the place, working to escape, but in the end, the sound was much a prisoner to the gloom, as I.

The supervising sky was littered with stars, but all the more dramatic for the garnish of nocturnal cloud play. Whispers of cirrus there, appeared captured in the spiral undertow of the earth, so that they were concentrated to a central point and spun outward in tapering dissolves. Together, those clouds and stars were the dusty pigments upon that celestial pinwheel of sky. What more perfectly impossible view could have been arranged as the backdrop for the unimaginable task before me: to capture and deliver the eclipsing moon? And, of that moon, he feared me not. Floating boldly a-sky, his paunch surged so near the earth, that the breeze of his rotation, bent the high grasses of the shore to his passing. Further sharpening his taunt, he appeared to hasten in pulling that ecliptic blanket across himself. The time was nigh, and I had none of it to waste.

I discovered that waiting just before my position, was the invite of a small, perfectly smooth stone. Surveying the whole of the lake's edge, that sole platform was the only break in the unending fence of lakeside vegetation. The tiny dock was not completely natural, but instead had been sculpted, so as to feature two soft grooves, perfect to accommodate both knees of one man kneeling. The stone was the equivalent of a park bench for the penitent reflector, who might visit that pond's sleek edge, seeking counsel upon its face. Placing my cane spear and dagger aside on the muddy shore, I knelt upon that fated stone and drank the medicine of that cup, which Pachamama had given me.

As the fingers of that rank sap ran down my throat, I was happily distracted by the luminous pond from that prostrate aspect. Had the situation not been so dire, I deemed that on that stone would have been a remarkable place, for it was imbued with a kind of magic, which gifted me the experience of feeling completely alone, and yet, with all the world. From that spot, the wonder of that gulf's power became clear. That aqueous canvass there, had magically coalesced the mise en scène of that wilderness and then polished it to an even finer finish. The final image reflected upon the surface there was impossibly superior to the original, which gave me pause as to which was reflection and which was source. In no instance I could recall, was an image cast by an object, greater than the image itself. I could think only of that aquaface, which left me to conclude that it was the lake was the source and all of creation around it, and the rest a mere reflection.

Though, Pachamama had made clear that I should abide, and allow for the medicine to provide its mysterious counsel, that moon was dissolving too quickly and a savage can hardly be called upon to wait. Every second past and yet another grain lost to forever, and so in that dearth of time and idea, I deemed my cane spear the best option. As much a fool's errand as it was, for what fool had ever thought to slay the moon, but ever worse, that same fool to think that his spear was the tool for such an enterprise. I considered my spear one last time, praying briefly upon it. Taking a few steps back from that water's edge, so as to provide the short runway, I surged the shore with maximum velocity and sent the pike into the lustrous firmament.

The length and form of my throw was the envy of King Arthur himself, as my spear, like Rhongomiant before it, made haste to the object of its slaying. As I watched it crossing that night sky, backlit by the jeering yellow moon, I was filled with a joyful memory of that virgin strike upon the jaguar. Just as the spike once hung between the great cat and me, so too did it then so hang 'tween man and moon. As the trajectory of the arrow dimmed, far, far short of that moon, it was swallowed hungrily by the cravat of murk, which nested the dark perimeter of the lake. I heard faintly, the splash of it, for it hadn't even cleared the lake itself. After a few moments, at the stone where I had knelt, came the rippling reports of my cane spear's final demise, into the sounding of those dark waters. Bitter-sweetness attended me quickly, realizing that strike or no, it was to be the last I would ever feel of that faithful pike in my fingers; a pike to which I owed much.

BINGE

Orangita III

Spearless and dejected, I stood to the ankles in that slick lake. As the waters resolved the echo of my pike's sad landing, they made prominent a collection of vines which were afloat in the shallows there. As the effects of that broth were taking hold in me, those vines appeared briefly as braids of those six maidens, creeping from shore to sea, so much so, that I searched the nearby darkness for the heads of those lovelies who had lent them.

Attending me, too, upon that cresting flush of medicine, was the cacophony of sounds, which dully caromed the place. The sounds of the forest whole, had become rich in my hearing. My eyes searched eagerly both the low and lofty place, where I was aware of every soughing. The iguana, whose underbelly was the percussion against the low dry grasses. The sound of gekkos and tree runners, as their tiny talons brushed the byways of tree bark. Across the center of that pond, I could even hear the surfacing boils of side-necked turtles, floating as moonlit dullards. Impossible, but true, even the mythic will o' the wisp, announced itself with a vacuumed whisper, from the far shore, bidding me lose myself to her. Owls calling to one another from wise perches, had drawn my limpid eyes skyward, where I discovered a hawk making passage across the sky, backlit by that eclipsing moon.

An idea! With my dagger, I cut a great rope of vine from beneath my feet, coiling it about my shoulder. Equipped with that length, I scampered from beachhead to branch, making quick work of ascending the towering tree over my position there. I moved with the adeptness of a capuchin, who lived aloft there, the lot of them admiring my ascent to the very crown. As I had done with the jaguar in the rescue of Jacob, I willed that hawk with my mind's eye, bidding him, meet me in the crown of that great tree. "Come!"

The hawk changed the direction of his flight, responding to my call, landing as a high companion, upon the branch adjacent.

"Hawk." said I, "Tonight it is you and I who must capture this great moon. You alone can aid me in this noble enterprise. You must take this length of vine and you must wrap it 'round that bastard moon, bringing it to me upon this string. Fly, now!"

The hawk took flight, sweeping a forked and short-winged arc for speed, dragging that vine so that it thinly disturbed the water's taught surface as it passed over lowly. With that momentum gained in his downward arc, he then ascended the night sky and I watched with bated breath. His wings out beating in the heavy rhythm of the large bird in flight, until he became a diminishing kite set against that moon's great torment. At last, I forfeited all view of him, and with it my very hopes, just as I had done upon the loss of that spear before him.

Upon that tactic's failure, my desperation crescendo'd. So little was the time I had left, and so outmatched was I by that glowering rotund. The inventory of my mind was spent, as an outturned and empty pocket. As well, my head was near fully surrendered to the power of Pachamama's mash. The combination of that perch and poison, gave me a high view of the lake's dark face. The colors upon that surface were melting and dancing before me, as the movement of those disturbed waters abetted the criminal moon, it's reflection then mocking me in hula.

Nothing left to do, but scream, I began a desperate howling to the whole of that dell, and to the sky even, bidding every creature to serve my will and sack that hovering moon. Within moments, the army of every living thing in the bush, all surged in stampede toward the crest of the hill, upon which that fat moon sat, as an over-dressed egg upon a high wall—waiting to be pushed. Every creature arrived in concert, upon that ripe hill, and their distant silhouettes became a row of carnival ducks upon a bowed horizon. In unison we cried out with the full pantheon of voice, becoming a wailing chorus, but the moon did not respond, only rejecting us incrementally with the indifferent advance of its shadowy cape.

Heart collapsed in my empty hand, I could not imagine a more difficult circumstance. As that very thought had been interpreted by Fate as a wish, there came a partner in the moon's resistance. A sudden and soldiering mist began to creep from the surrounding murk and over the entire face of the lake. It came, and it came from all sides, approaching as a tightening collar, from every shore into the lake's raven center. As the creeping circumference of that mist finally imploded where it gathered, it sent skyward a fat tower of white vapor. As it reached its apex, the vaporous column spilled over itself, forming an ever expanding mushroom cloud, as it was picked up by the high breezes over the entirety of the place.

As it consumed the life it drifted over, even in my high place, I became part of its nosh. There inside that menacing vapor, was the smell of every dead thing, as if it was not fog, but a poison come to exterminate the lot of us. Upon that far horizon, where my faithful forest companions had bayed the moon for me, the animals were expiring at right angles where they stood, upon contact with that mortal mist. Even as I surveyed the very branches of my tree, searching for my capuchin monkeys, I found them falling as rag dolls, the sound of their descent, the dull thumping of corpses against the arms and floors of the forest. That death vapor had come to exterminate the memory of every living thing in its radius.

I was overtaken by the density of dread within that billowing death, seeing too that the full moon had been blotted out by him. My eyes were to stinging and my lungs burned with that same thinly fire, which glazed them beneath the ground in that clearing. As high above the earth as I was, I was buried alive, once again, by that deadly mist. The shortness of breath…the constriction of throat, all echoes to that episode in the clearing. How far I had come and only to die in that same manner I had so earlier escaped.

Those symptoms and the profound loss of that eclipsing devil were too much to bear. I could not return empty handed, nor could I face the slow and impending doom in that death vapor. As I inventoried the place for any sign of life, the sights and the sounds, which had attended me there, had all been dissolved in the very spot of their last standing. Only I was left to survey that comprehensive field of death.

I walked the plank of that tree's high branch, so desperate was I to end the profound emptiness and solitude upon that earth. Without pause, I reached the end of that yielding branch and leapt in a suicidal swan dive into the thick plume of that vapor, awaiting impact in the shallows below. Instead, I was met with a great depth in that water, which spared me, unmercifully. My fall had merely disturbed the great cloak of fog, and nothing else, so that I came to find I had arrived right back at the shore, where that quiet stone was waiting, having completed some deathly circle. Alone again in that spot, I was so afraid. I tell you, I have never been so afraid.

Desperate, kneeling again upon that stone, though drenched, I cried into the face of the lake, "Dark lake, dark lake, tell me, what is it I must do?! What must I know, so that I may finally die? I don't desire to live one single moment more. Please erase me from this place, from this earth, so that I may rest, at last!"

My tears fell upon the face of that water, which worked to clear away a small wreath of space, so that I had clear view mirrored beneath it. I leaned out over the water, from my kneeling position, and gained view of myself. Mine was still the face, though the melting face, of the night sky. The pigments upon me were running away, so that I was unmasked, as it were. "If I am not this great hunter, Orion, then, lake, who am I?!

What, what is to become of me?!"

I disturbed the surface of the water with my hand and waited for it to settle again. I could see a pale light from the depths, growing brighter, until an image began to appear...

CHAPTER 31

BE

was then to witness to a morbid parade of faces, which changed one to another, without evidence of the scenes between them. The first that shimmered in the depth was the face of the old woman who had been buried beside me in the clearing, she was the same from whom I had inherited the Saint Christopher medallion. As she smiled up to me so warmly, she appeared so much alive there under the water.

A wonderful coal was lit at the center of my chest, which is that incomparable symptom of love which flickers, when we remember those we've lost.

She was my grandmother, Muzzy, who was that immovable affection in my impossible childhood. She raised the Saint Christopher medallion from about her neck, kissed it once and smiled to me through the aquaface. I was lost in the magic of seeing her there, so real, which left me unprepared for the change which overtook her suddenly. Without warning, her face was replaced by the head of that great black jaguar, who had drowned beneath those falls. I reached into the water to rescue my grandmother, screaming, "Noooooooooo!" My hands returned empty, finding no substance in the shoal.

The water settled again and yet, another face began emerging there. As it became clear, it was the face of that pilot, my father, looking up to me. He was that granite countenance, as he raised his index finger to his lips, in the manner of a hushing me, and in his gentle voice which came rising through the surface there, saying, "Time and forgetting, Christopher. Time and forgetting. Time and forgetting." I blinked away fierce tears from my eyes, my heart in a tangle in my chest. As I was responding to him, before even the slightest utterance, his head, too, replaced by that menacing skull of the great black cat. Again, I plunged my fist into those waters, but there was nothing beneath the surface, but all the more of that water itself. I was mad; mad from the mix of that swill and that death vapor which had consumed all but me, in that landscape.

And with that resignation from sanity, a final face did appear in the shallows. It was the most wrenching of all, for it was the face of Jacob, as he slept, as I had seen him in that veil of such innocence. I was reminded of the sweetness and goodness and faithfulness of him, but it was then rushed with panic, for fear of that cat's return to claim him. "Run, Jacob! Go! Run that cat comes for you!" I screamed into the surface. And, again that blasphemous cat's head appeared upon the body of that little boy. My hands again plumed the waters, wrestling for the head of that beast who was claiming those who deserved it least.

I cried to the heavens, "What is this?! Why, why do you torture me thus?! How I suffer and suffer again, you show me those whom I have lost! I say to you, dark lake, you are a motherless whore! And, I am the savage who fears you not!"

Upon my outburst, those torturing waters became ominously still, erasing every ghostly reflection. That death vapor which had consumed the whole of that lake and its surround, retreated as if a cover being pulled from a mattress. Left in the wake, were the fat moon above, which had nearly turned to blood, and me upon my knees over that water's face. Waiting.

As I stared deeply into the darkness of that pond, another image did finally begin to emerge, though it was not delivered in a plume of light, as the others had been. This, instead, was the dark, dark face, surfacing from the very depth. As it arrived to rest, just the other side of that liquid pane, it was the face of that same jaguar, whom I had spared upon the high falls.

As I studied the every chisel of his face from the safe vantage of mere memory, he returned his deep gaze back to me, his deepset amber eyes as magnificent jewels set in the onyx of his head. His eyes were hypnotic on me, whether real or ghost, I was lost to him.

Suddenly, a terrific roar rose from those depths and without warning that great beast surged from beneath that surface, crashing through the plate of that lake The jaguar, in full flight of ambush, had leapt upon me, pinning me to the earth and rearing back its ferocious head.

I wrestled from him, as best I could, but it was the great advantage to him. I could not find clearance, but only became lost, and more lost in the density of his coat, which was as a hot rug which muted the air about me, until I was suffocating. He drew his head back and revealed the eyed teeth, dripping were they with his spit and desire, and then he plunged at my face repeatedly, missing me for my ability to roll just the centimeters required.

I was far too weak, too weak in that congested position, my muscles trembling to the fatigue and the great weight and force upon me. At last, the muscles of my back and shoulders were threads, which left me surrendering to his overwhelming force.

I wanted no more of that life in the jungle, in that endless fight for survival. There was only the final test of my fidelity to those cries which I had made for my own end. With that, I yielded completely to the monster, laying back my heavy head, so as to expose the ripe vein of my neck, for him to claim. I cried out, "Take me, you beast! Free me from the torture of this eclipse!"

Upon my command, tapers of spit falling from his eyed teeth, he reared back his great mouth and with plunging force struck me one last time. My body convulsed wildly, shuddering from the force of his final strike. I awaited the sting of his mouth upon my neck, but after a long moment, there was no pain at all. There was no sound. There was not the hot breath from that beast upon me any longer. I blinked my eyes into a disbelieving and open state, to behold: The Jaguar had vanished! There was no sign of him, whatever. There, upon that ground, there was only I, lying in a prostrate heap, breathing wildly and surveying the surroundings. He was gone.

I scrambled, broken into a hundred pieces, back to that kneeling stone, to search for that vanished in the deep. Cautiously, I peered over the edge to behold what face would come. As the waters there settled, I awaited the view of my own melting face or that jaguar ascending again from that deep. I was not prepared for what I beheld there, for it was no place in my knowing. The reflection that waited there for me, was that of my own body, donning the full head of that black cat!

The longer I stared, the more I allowed for my trembling hands to survey my own skull, the more each moment confirmed it was true, that I was the body of man, and the head of beast!

I fell upon my back, scrambling desperately from that shoreline, for I could drink no more images from that lake. I had peered out upon the wider lake there, then quieting as I studied it, my eyes met by that eclipsing moon, casting its liquefied reflection, as blood over that water's face.

Blood, over the water's face. The liquefied moon! It was all there, all along, it had been before my very eyes, hidden from my mind! There, next to that kneeling stone, was the empty cup, from which I had drunk the medicine upon my first arrival there. That shimmering column of The Blood Moon, reflected moonlight, providing a path to that waiting cup!

I collected the cup into my trembling hands and dipped it furiously into that water. Raising the cup to my eyes, I beheld, that liquid moon therein, the prisoner of that simple wooden cup!

I howled at the smug moon, "I've got you now, you bastard! The blood of you now dances in this cup of mine!"

It was as Pachamama had said it would be, for it was not the warrior who had slain the moon, but the poet, instead.

BINGE

CHAPTER 32

TIME AND FORGETTING

istinct and wonderful are the clouds of dust, which can be seen beneath the feet of the distant messengers, who bear happy news. Such was the plumage beneath my every step returning back to the garden. My hands were equally engaged, solely chartered to keep stable and cover, the wooden cup, which was my precious cargo. Shepherding me along that path returning, was a brightly dancing Sherpa, who had arrived in the form of a butterfly. Whether leading me with intention or merely a fellow traveler upon the same path of jungle, he proved a happy kite for those thousand steps returning.

As was revealed upon my arrival to the garden, it was not Pachamama alone who waited, but those darling nymphs, as well, who had prepared me for the hunt. The joyful mood of we two arriving, that butterfly and me, was in stark contrast to their lamenting voices, which produced the very song of sorrow; a quiet seriously miscast score beneath my triumphant return.

They were oblivious to my arrival, or they didn't care, so deeply involved were they in mourning. The seven were collected over the banks of that depleted stream, and beneath that bloody moon, which hung so menacingly above them. Beneath them, I could see that that former river had been reduced to a mere streamlet, nearly dead, it was.

"Maidens, what is this song of sorrow you sing? For, your Orion has returned."

As Pachamama turned to face me, she was crestfallen. Her maidens, a weeping chorus, drifted in rank behind her, as she approached me.

"My dear, Orion, I can see by that cat's head upon your shoulders, that you have been slain beneath this blood moon. Such a waste. I knew the task impossible, when I asked it of you, but, I believed it had been written."

"But, my darling, why do you all weep so, upon my return? Have you no faith, in you dear Orion? Can you not see the lightness in my being, as I return?"

Pachamama, depressedly responded, "We see only the trickle of this dying stream, which is moments from its end, as well as this blood moon still hung in the heavens. You return to us with empty hands, save the very cup, which I sent with you."

"No, Pachamama, you don't understand. You mustn't despair, for I have done it!"

"Orion, you clearly have NOT done it, for it is the moon you were to bring me, and yet it still hangs in the heavens."

"You were right, Pachamama. You were right about all of it. That I was called. That the medicine would allow me to see what I was blind to all along. That it would be the poet and not the warrior, who captured this Blood Moon."

She and the band of maids were a collective of confusion, for though the dawn of hope was rising in their eyes, as I gathered them 'round me.

"Let me show you, my darlings. Let me show you this Blood Moon, which I have brought to you in this very garden."

My hand remained over the top of the cup, so as not to spill a drop from it. I moved to the midst of those shadows cast by the towering Tree of Life, so that we shared a space where the moon's pale red glow shone fully, unobstructed.

"You have asked me to hunt and capture this blood moon. I swear to you, I thought the task impossible. I exhausted every method I could think of, until I admit, I was well defeated and prepared to die. But, there upon that dark shore, the answer did appear to me so clearly, that I knew at once the answer had been written...on my very heart."

Their attention was focused fully upon the cup, which was centered in our huddle. With all eyes on that single spot, I removed my hand from the cup to reveal its contents: a brimming challis of liquid moonlight, which danced therein.

Pachamama was stunned, as she beheld the simple, but miraculous, occupant in that vessel.

"You see him?! He is there, Pachamama! For, I have delivered the mass of him in this water, which contains him, so that he may never escape from it!"

She beheld in wonder, transfixed, though clearly uncertain of the deed's completion.

"Orion, can this be? We must know for certain that this answer is true."

She bent down to the ground, from which she collected one of those thousands of expired chrysalis from the tree of life.

She put the withered pod into her palm and then dipped her finger into that moonlit cup, retrieved a single drop, which hung on her index. The drop of water lengthened and finally fell upon that long dead pod.

As we all watched in wonder, the tiny pod was transformed from that beige color of death and into an emerald green, so rich and vital, it was the envy of every living thing aforest. It then began its rocking wildly in her palm, cracking suddenly, as something was emerging from therein. Pachamama's eyes misted over, as she beheld that chrysalis finally breaking, from which emerged the great miracle of life, which is the butterfly!

The tiny newborn, rose up in our midst and circled us, its wings aflutter, dancing upon the thermals of our collective joy. And then, as we watched, that butterfly landed upon my very shoulder.

"You, see, Pachamama! It is true, this water which is the moon which you have sought so long, which will deliver this new life you have been seeking!"

She was overflowing in joy, "It is true! It is true! There's no time to waste, it for the blood moon is nearly past."

She took the cup carefully from my hands and made haste down the banks of that dying river, which had been reduced to a mere trickle. Looking to the heavens, she cried out,.. *"This cup, which is the cup of pure consciousness, contains within its walls, the imprisoned moon. It has been written that this one* who *would come, who would capture this moon, and rescue this stream and all that feeds from it. I make this offering of forgiveness, in this act of freeing this captured moon, into this dying stream!"*

With that, Pachamama poured forth from the small cup, that liquid moonlight. As the waters spilled into that dying river, the river did surge immediately. From the length of it upstream; from beneath the very floor of it; and even from a great rain, which fell suddenly from the moonlit heavens, that river rose in mere moments, so that it nearly crested its own banks. Restored.

The nymphets had gathered, clinging to me in a frenzy. Pachamama took my face into her hands, saying, "Savage, you are him who has been chosen, for no man has done this but you. Come, let us away, for your inheritance awaits."

The darlings and I followed Pachamama to the bowl of that Tree of Life. As we entered there, all eight of us, I was confronted by a most unexpected bed chamber. Save the pure loveliness of those nubile maids, the room was furnished only by two great heaps of bones.

Pachamama, moving with the ease of unconscious beauty, took quickly her place upon the bed made of skulls. There were hundreds of them, craniums, which formed a macabre mattress.

The sextet moved to the opposing pile of bones, upon which they lay in every seductive posture. That bed, however, was not a bed of skulls, but rather, a small hill of fossilized phalluses. There were dozens and dozens of those expired members, which shaped that alternate bed. The nymphs and queens had been sorted, as it were.

"Pachamama, I am confused by these bones. Who has made this bed, upon which these perfect darlings writhe?"

"Imposters." she said, nonplussed.

"And you..? This bed you sleep upon, which is this bed of skulls, who has made this bed for you?"

"Time has made this bed savage. We have made it together, Time and me. You have been chosen, my darling savage. And, now, it is you who must choose."

"Choose? Pachamama, you can see that I am so happy and yet, greatly confused."

The lusty nymphs had made easy work of drawing me into their scrum. Their wet lips, lithe shanks, copper bellies and darling braids, had become the risen tide of all things feminine and powerful, up to the neck of me. There in the midst of them, upon that bed of cocks, they each focused only upon me, as they began releasing their darling braids, until I was awash in an ocean of their hair around me; a helpless Pisces, trapped in the Aquarian net. My loins raged, as their hungry hands and mouths traveled the whole of my broken body in lusty enterprise.

Pachamama rose from her bed, approaching. "This choice before you, savage, is not simple. You have suffered greatly on this journey, even unto your dying in the fangs of the black beast. You have expired and experienced the depths of fear... for the greatest pains of loss...the agony of physical torment... and, at last, even your very mind was made a knot by this moon. You have rarely known a moment's peace."

As she watched me, drowning in those feverish nymphs, she retrieved a clay carafe, pouring it a stream of something, which looked the spitting image of mercury, into that cup which held the moon.

"You must choose. You may take of either of these and do so freely and without explanation. Any decision need only be understood by you. You may taste of these maidens in orgy with them. Upon your very climax, you will be delivered painlessly entering a dreamless sleep, which will deliver you from the suffering. This choice will take you from this world of consciousness, recycling your soul, stripping it of memory, and redeploy it into another life."

"The peace that comes in death, then?"

"Indeed. You will not be alone, for others have chosen that relief of death, which has built that phallic pile, upon which you orgy."

"My other option?"

She moved to me, with the cup, which she had poured.

"In this cup, is the water from that stream, which is pure consciousness. You may, instead, drink of this cup fulfilling your calling, join us as one of The Chosen. If you drink of this cup, however, you will never die. Forever, you shall live. And, forever, is a time filled with pain and suffering and loss, which is all that you have suffered the way till now."

"Who is a man who can live forever? Does this water preserve the body of a man from decay and death?"

"When I say 'you' will live forever, I am not speaking of the body, but of the mind. The body is matter and it will decay. The law of nature it is written. But, 'you' are not this body, but this 'mind', which occupies this body, as the caterpillar occupies the chrysalis, where it becomes the very butterfly, which sits upon your shoulder."

"How is this possible then, to live forever, if the body will die?"

"You asked, who made this bed of mine and I told you that it is Time and ME, who have made this bed of skulls. Each of these, which I now rest upon, is a life, which has past. These are my own bones, which I have left behind, as I have moved my consciousness forward from one form to the next."

"You have died these hundreds times, which are easily the number of skulls which make this bed?"

"It is as you say. But, upon the effect of drinking directly from this stream of pure consciousness, it is not merely the consciousness, which travels forward, but all of the wisdom, memory, learning, grief, joy, pain, exhilaration and loss. All move forward, as the energy of the soul separates from the matter of the body."

"If this is so, Pachamama, how ancient you are. And, how much you must know."

"These skulls tell the story of a woman, who saw the world when it first began."

"What, what is the profit for a man who lives forever? If there is this suffering and dying and living again, only to suffer and die, is not the suffering too great? For a man will never escape his pain, without time and forgetting."

"Time and Forgetting, yes. It is the doubled edged sword, is this Time and Forgetting. It is the time and forgetting, which make us sick, which sickness can only be healed by more time and forgetting. It is both the poison and the cure. A burden to be sure. However, these few of us, who have chosen this path of consciousness, are these few who change the world. The man who cures the dreadful disease. The woman who lives in this very garden, as steward of consciousness. The philosopher who changes the thoughts. The artist who interprets the transcendent for the masses. I say, even this very poet before me, who dared to capture the moon, at no profit to himself, but for the world. These are the benefits, which may make the burden almost possible to bear."

"And, you are saying that if I choose to drink of this cup...?"

"You will live to change and shape and even save creation. The choice is yours alone."

The maidens were at work over the whole of me and I had done enough fighting. When I surrendered myself to that black cat, I did so with the call for my own death in that jungle. I was tired and craved that rest and peace, which would come.

They swarmed me and I happily dissolved into the warmth of that united flesh. I was happily surrendering to the sweet taste of them, each. Their lips...their hair...their dazzling eyes and their desire, raining down upon me and I, happily drowning. Death in the fangs of that great beast brought the promise of final agony. But, to die, at last, in the midst of that bevy, was an easy passing into a permanent peace.

"Shall I join you in that bed then..?" Pachamama asked, her eyes jeweled like a fire into her very soul. She extended her languid hand, putting down the cup, so as to join the orgy and deliver me to the ecstasy of that final peace. In her opposite hand, away from the hoard of us, she held the cup.

"Come to me, Pachamama, and join in this final consumption, my darling. For all I desire is the feel you all these upon me, one last time, and then to be delivered into that final peace, which will end this long, long suffering."

I led her into the hoard, taking her hand and dissolving into her great mouth as she arrived. The orgy had reached its pitch, as Pachamama took the great shaft of me and guided it to her sex. In a blind fit, I freed myself, scrambling free of the octopussy, grabbed that wooden cup and eagerly drank of it!

"I am sorry and I am not sorry, my darlings. For, what point was there in all the suffering, if I hadn't used it to make something better?"

I fell to the floor, collapsed, as that liquid delivered me to a wonderful... heaviness.

CHAPTER 33

PRECIOUS CARGO

 was a prisoner of deep sleep, only the least bit of consciousness having diluted an otherwise perfect leaden state. I hovered there in lucidity, as long as I was able, a discipline that I had hard won through a life committed to oversleep. As if a sun cresting the eastern horizon, my wakefulness appears to me as a precise and thin horizon of light, projected upon the interior of my closed lids. At last, that golden thread of light dissolves, as if it were a filament of sugar, consumed by an ever inferior alertness.

On that morning, I had landed deftly on the image of myself as a waiting butterfly, still encased within its chrysalis, inverted in a high corner, which I thought reserved for cobwebs and long legged spiders alone. From the inside of that cozy den, I could hear the voice of a woman, speaking gently to another occupant in the room.

"Sir, it's been quite some time. We really must move the body from here."

There was no response from the man to whom she was speaking.

Patiently, she offered, "Well, a few more minutes, I suppose. I'll just leave you alone, then. Again, I'm so sorry for your loss."

I then felt the walls of my tiny prison fracturing, accommodating the stretch of me, until at last, the shell opened and I emerged, my wings falling heavily over my inverted head. From that overturned aspect, I blinked into focus and could see Anunk, that wonderful main of yellow white hair and the marvelous darkness of his face. His eyes were keenly upon my emergence, without the least bit turning, willing me from that tiny sock.

Behind Anunk, I could see the corpse, laying in that bed near that window, enjoying the dreamless sleep, which the dead alone may know. The face upon that expired body, was my own face, which I had lived behind for forty years till then. And, of course, that body too, which evidenced the ravages to its every cell, by the cancer which occupied its throat.

But, as I looked upon myself there, lifeless, I was no longer seeing 'me', but the shell of me. The body there and it was no less the chrysalis than that from which I had just emerged, as a butterfly. For, as Pachamama had taught me, the body dies away, but the soul simply changes form...redeployed to new purpose. And, I thought, dead as it was, such a body might still be of some use.

Anunk held up his hand to me, calling for my descent to the perch of his ancient finger. I released myself from that high corner, fluttering down to meet him, my thin wings delivering me to that wonderful, new lightness of being. I landed safely, following that virgin flight, there upon Anunk's finger, as he retrieved that giant cigar of his. He blew another of those great brumes of smoke over the whole of me, the heat moving easily through my translucent wings. He put his opposite hand on that lifeless corpse, there in the bed, and I felt suddenly strange, as if I were sand moving through a straw, from the delicate frame of the butterfly and back into the body from whence I had come.

The weight above my yearning face was but a veil, as some cool provision of air found me. With one final stretch from that darkness, I at last breached the chrysalis and took a deep plunging breath! As soon as the first provision of oxygen made its way through my wilted esophagus, it was urgently distributed to the outskirts of me.

As I blinked into consciousness, my eyes beheld him there. The man who was a shocking sight in any land, but his own, for there was no negotiating one's eyes from that great mane, which had never known the sweep of brush or comb or shear. Anunk held my face in his ancient hands, adjusting it so that my eyes were completely locked with his.

"Anunk...?" I whispered.

"Tiger, you return. You have drunk of the cup. Welcome."

"Is it…is it real, Anunk? Am I…?"

"Did you find the little boy?"

"I did. In a, a crashed plane, Anunk, I found him."

"And, your mother and father?"

"How can know these things, which were hidden even from me? I did find them, both. I forgave, Anunk. I did nothing but forgive."

"This is all there is, Tiger. Forgiveness. Our thoughts are things. And these thoughts, are those which became this cancer in your throat. This cancer which is gone from you now."

"But, I died, Anunk. Or, was it a dream? There was the most beautiful butterfly. I did die, right?"

BINGE

"Sleep now, Tiger. For the man who drinks of the cup, is the man who has much time for doing. But, for now, this man, he must sleep."

He collected his few things, placing them back into his haversack. Amongst the items were that cigar and the little wooden cup. He picked up his long cane instrument, which rivaled him in height. As he prepared to leave, he kissed me on the forehead and made way for the door. As he passed the end of my bed, he stopped briefly and held up his closed hand. Staring at me intently, he opened his fingers as the petals of a flower, to reveal that marvelous butterfly, hidden in his palm! Smiling to me, he placed the tiny creature upon the post at the end of my bed.

"It was real! Anunk? It was real!"

"I will be waiting, when you are ready, Tiger. We only have... forever, hmmm."

With that, he unceremoniously drifted from the room, leaving me alone, abed. Passing him as he left, was that gentle nurse, who entered the room to find me very much and very unexpectedly alive. She reacted in the appropriate horror and excitement, then running down the hallway screaming for my doctors.

As I lay there, in that gloom of chartreuse, which is the color of fluorescent lights upon indifferent walls, I was captive to that wonderful butterfly, upon that post at the end of my bed. As I stared at him, I willed him gently, 'Come." He rose, then, and fluttered about me, a brightly dancing Sherpa. He then drifted out the open window at my bedside, and into the waiting Spring. As I watched him disappearing, another of those gentle breezes came to comfort me, delivering upon it, a thousand tiny treasures...

𝕭𝖎𝖓𝖌𝖊

Glossary

embering	*Verb*—Process where wood or charcoal is dissolving to a white hot ember
grainless	*Adj.*—Without grain
esses	Plural of the letter "S"
volars	*Noun*—Relating to the palm of the hand or the sole of the foot.
ceremonialized	*Verb*—Made significant or ritualized
necrophilial	*Adj.*—Physical attraction to a corpse
viridescent	*Adj.*—Shimmering and massive wall of green
deepset	*Adj.* -embedded or positioned firmly or deeply.
strandedness	*Adj*—Describes a state of being isolated or completely abandoned
razored	*Adj.*—Describes the sharpness of an edge
fan brush	*Noun*—A wide brush painters use in the painting of landscapes
serpentined	*Adj.*—Winding or 'snaking'

BINGE

pungence	*Adj.*—The quality of odor/odor that stings the nose, said especially of acidic or spicy substances
gristling	*Adj.*—The grinding sound of bone and ligament being separated
sabled	*Adj.*—Black and course hair
hakenkreuz	*Noun*—German word for Swastika;
wagger	*Noun*—A tail
bonelessness	*Adj.*—Without bones, as with a snake
vom tag	*Adj.*—Describing a posture used in sword fighting, where the hands are high above the head, readying for a downward strike. Literally, "from the roof"
detrusion	*Verb*—thrusting outward or downward
leviathine	*Adj.*—a monstrous object
invertical	*Adj.*—a degree of vertical angle that is so great that it inverts to a negative slope
opaqued	*Verb*—became semi-translucent
diagonaled	*Adj*—a line cutting across an axis at a 45 degree angle
treeline	*Noun*—The horizon created by the tops of a group of trees

lumpishly	*Adj.*—to move like an oaf; heavy footed; uncommitted
balded	*Adj.*—Having little or no hair on the scalp
Rastafarian	*Adj.*—Describes physical appearance, especially related to dreadlocks
octopussed	*Adj.*—To hold on or fasten with all limbs
forlorned	*Adj.*—Pitifully sad and abandoned or lonely
grafittied	*Adj.*—Something which has been written upon
awestruckedly	*Adv.*—Old English; describing the observation of something overwhelming to the senses
grande	*Adj.*—French; description of a large sweeping motion in ballet
à terre	*Noun*—French; a dance movement where one is returned to earth from flight
cursived	*Adj.*—Describing an elegant and sweeping motion
en avant	*Verb*—French; a dance movement that requires the dancer to move forward

Weisslacker	*Noun*—A German cheese
nostrilled	*Noun*—past tense; consumed through the nose/nostril
discreting	*Verb*—Hiding
Sighingly	*Adv.*—acceptance after exhaustion
mitred	*Adj.*—having been cut or split
spake	*Verb*—past tense of speak; Old English form
Vergeben	*Noun*—German word for Forgiveness
uncried	*Adj.*—Tears which have not yet been shed
Erste	*Noun*—German word for First
Zweiter	*Noun*—German word for Second
sinewed	*Adj.*—Describes the appearance of fluidity or flexibility
audiomist	*Noun*—Sound which rises and settles over an area
assholed	Adj.—An object that is placed inside of the ass
headly	*Adj.*—Pertaining to the head
aquafury	*Noun*—The force of raging waters, as in waterfalls

aquafjord	*Noun*—A waterfall which falls at a perfect right angle to a river, creating a sheer cliff
aquaface	*Noun*—Reflective water created by surface tension
waitingly	*Adv.*—An object or person positioned to wait patiently for certain arrival
Monet'ed	*Adj.*—Referring to the French painter Oscar-Claude Monet.
discreted	*Adv.*—Hidden from view
torsioned	*Verb*—Twisting and elongating of the torso
rifflers	*Noun*—A narrow elongated tool with a curved file surface at each end, used in filing concave surfaces.
hairlined	*Adj.*—Describing a field of hair
poreless	*Adj.*—Skin without pores; perfectly smooth and unblemished
centerpoint	*Noun*—The mathematical center of a circle
Punraz'	*Noun*—Word stemming from a Common Germanic *Þunraz (meaning "God of thunder")

BINGE

hueless	*Adj.*—Without color
mélange	*Noun*—French word for 'soup'
nubiles	*Noun*—Young and free spirited women
glycerined	*Adj.*—Shiny, slick and/or glistening
helixed	*Adj.*—Winding around a center column
spectre	*Noun*—an object in focus
indigoed	*Adj.*—painted deep blue
wainscoting	*Noun*—paneling
pishtaq	*Noun*—Islamic architecture, a rectangular frame around an arched opening, usually associated with an iwan
Rebenesque	*Adj.*—Full figured
Betelgeuse, Rigel, Saiph, Trapezium Cluster, Alnitak, Alnilam, Mintaka, Meissa and Bellatrix	*Noun*—Critical stars that form the prominent constellation Orion located on the celestial equator which is visible throughout the world. It is one of the most recognizable constellations in the night sky, named after Orion, a hunter in Greek mythology.
vajeen	*Noun*—Vagina
o'ertaken	*Adv.*—Old English, stylized spelling of 'overtaken'

foliole	*Adj.*—Having to do with trees and/or leaves
mise en scène	*Noun*—"mise en scene' refers to the total atmosphere that is established as an event is to happen
Rhongomiant	*Noun*—("little white hilt"), was the dagger of King Arthur in the Welsh Arthurian legends. It is sometimes attributed with the magical power to shroud its user in shadow
Spearless	*Adj.*—Without spear
gekkos	*Noun*—Plural; Gekko is a genus of Southeast Asian geckos, commonly known as true geckos or calling geckos, in the family Gekkonidae
crescendo'd	*Adj.*—Climaxed
depressedly	*Adv.*—acting within a depressed state or as one who is depressed
aforest	*Adv.*—Within the forest
chrysalis	*Noun*—the hard outer case enclosing a chrysalis
octopussy	*Noun*—An orgy of woman characterized by no less than four

𝖇𝖎𝖓𝖌𝖊

ACKNOWLEDGEMENTS

Knowing the written word is a lost art form and there are not enough pleases and thank yous in this world today. I would like to thank the following: Muzzy and Gramps for having my mother Grange Margret Rutan and Ramona and Josip for having Captain Joseph Leonard Mahne, and to both of them for bringing me into this lifetime, along with my precious sister Grangey and my second father Rolf Gunther Habermann for loving me too, thank you for being.

To the many beautiful people of my blessed life, to all the women I have loved, my beloved Tigress whoever she might be, and to all the haters who have taught me LOVE is the greatest gift of all, I love you all...

To all the medicines of the Amazon in particular Ayahuasca and Yagé, and for Pachamama, and the universe for creating these medicines. To the many shamans, Taitas, and medicine men and women who have served these medicines, in particular Don José Campos, Alfredo Zagaceta, Taita Gerardo, Porfidio, Taita Juanito, Carlos and Brad. Along with the entire medicine community for which I have shared space with, thank you for being, I love you all...

To all of the wonderful people that have helped me put this project together; Samantha Scott a.k.a. Sam I Am Photography for her photograph that was used for the cover of this book, Estevan Oriol for his support and photography and his introduction to Mister Cartoon, you too Angel, Cartoon for my tattoos and for his creating the lettering of *Lives and Minds of C.W. Männe* BINGE, you too Hunter for following up with all the digital file versions, Grangita for her one of a kind original drawings, Erin Tyler for being able to combine all of the elements into one Baddd Ass cover, spine and back cover, and last but not least: Sir David Michael Robinson, my brother from another, not only for his friendship of over 25 years, but also for him being able to channel this story into an epic masterpiece, thank you for being, I love you all…

𝕭𝕴𝕹𝕲𝕰

ABOUT
THE AUTHORS

Christopher William Mahne a.k.a. C.W. Männe, started this journey some almost 50 years ago as a little boy just being. That little boy had tragedies and triumphs as he followed his path to manhood. It wasn't until he did the 12 steps of AA and got sober that his mind had the clarity to want more, heal more, be more and love more. After gaining sobriety, he sought out many spiritual masters who led him to meditation and to ponder 'who am I?'

Thereafter, he found the ancient medicines of Ayahuasca and Yagé, that changed his life forever. This is his story of that haunting and beautiful path to drink from the cup of 'pure consciousness.'

Sir David Michael Robinson, has spent over two decades working as a screenwriter, novelist and poet. Robinson's work is the result of twin influences: his formal religious training at seminary and his study of world mythologies. Under the strong influence of teacher Joseph Campbell, he is preoccupied with the discovery of "the hero with a thousand faces," and mankind's search for universal truth. His chronicling the extraordinary real life of C.W. Männe is the result of over twenty five years of observation, collaboration and friendship. He lives with his wife, LB, and four children in San Clemente, California.

ABOUT GRANGITA'S

Grangita's are a plethora, actually an ethos of 18 black and white minuets exclusively created and designed by the Grange spirit herself to portray *Lives and Minds of C.W. Männe* BINGE not in words, but in one-of-a-kind Grangita's. Each one has a mind and spirit of its own to let the viewer's mind run wild with what if? story imagery; the pure and simple truth of Grangita's, is to unlock the inner reality and spirit of us all.

To be continued...